DASHBURY PARK

HEIR to the Dashbury estates and title, Ludovic comes over from Italy to visit his uncle, the present peer. Despite the efforts of his grandmother and his cousin Lucy, Ludovic soon tires of the settled routine of an English landed estate. His unusual childhood—his father, a much-travelled diplomat who had married a great Austrian beauty—makes him feel more at home in cosmopolitan Rome than on his ancestral acres. It takes the bitterness of an unhappy love affair and the example of Lucy's engagement to make Ludovic realise where his duty lies and hearken to the promptings of his own heart.

Dashbury Park reconstructs a vanished way of life. The Victorian age is so completely and precisely visualised that its tears and laughter—its boredoms and frustrations too—can be felt again across the years. Susan Tweedsmuir's world—so near to ours in time but so remote from ours in spirit—sets off to perfection her intensely human story of conflict between duty and self-interest.

Susan Tweedsmuir's own childhood was spent at the great Palladian mansion of Moor Park, in Hertfordshire, her family home. She married John Buchan in 1905.

By the same author

"An achievement little short of astonishing—an evocation not merely of the patterns of behaviour and modes of thought of the high Victorian era, but of its most intimate, tender and courageous spirit. It gives off the perfume of a vanished age.

"Many other books make a deal more clamour; few, I think, will remain longer in the thankful memory." JOHN CONNELL *(Evening News)*.

"Cousin Harriet adds to its other merits deep background and thoroughly well-built plot." ELIZABETH BOWEN *(Tatler)*.

"A beautifully constructed story, neatly characterized and altogether credible. Miss Austen would have found much to approve and little to criticize in Lady Harriet Waveney." *The Times.*

DASHBURY PARK

A Victorian Story

by

SUSAN TWEEDSMUIR

GERALD DUCKWORTH & CO. LTD
3 Henrietta Street, London, W.C.2

First published 1959

© SUSAN LADY TWEEDSMUIR, 1959

PRINTED IN GREAT BRITAIN BY
WESTERN PRINTING SERVICES LIMITED BRISTOL

To my historian friends

GEORGE GLAZEBROOK
and
A. L. ROWSE

*I dedicate this book to you both as a small token of my
gratitude for all the kindness you have shown to me about
my writing. I lived as a child in the late Victorian era
in a house somewhat like the one I describe, and I hope
that this eye-witness account of days so unlike the times
we live in now may have some interest to you and to my
readers.*

With affection
SUSAN TWEEDSMUIR

Kennst du das Haus? Auf Säulen ruht sein Dach,
Es glänzt der Saal, es schimmert das Gemach,
Und Marmorbilder stehn und sehn mich an:

GOETHE

One does not love a place the less from having
suffered in it.

JANE AUSTEN

1

TEA was just beginning at Dashbury Park. The heavily brocaded curtains were hanging undrawn. The fire had been banked up into a noble blaze. The round tea table was spread with a white cloth and if a tea table could be said to groan it should have emitted a distressed sound.

The Dashbury family sat round looking at the plates of bread and butter, scones, the translucent jams and the massive uncut cakes.

Lady Dashbury sat behind an embossed silver tea urn grasping the handle of a teapot, also embossed, which matched the urn.

"It is just light enough," she said, "to have tea by daylight. I always hope it will be on your mother's birthday."

Her sister-in-law said nothing and the other members of the group round the tea table received this remark in silence. The youngest member of the party stood by Lady Dashbury handing the cups round to the assembled company. She paused, cup in hand, and looked out through the tall windows; dusk was gathering round the house, but the stone urns on the terrace were still visible and there was a hint that more than a month after the shortest day (on January twentieth in fact), the lightening and loosening up of winter was beginning.

As Lucy Taynton laid down her cup beside the plate Lady Dashbury said,

7

"Lucy, you're dreaming, you'll spill your tea."

Lucy started and sat down abruptly, but her eyes again sought the soft dusk outside.

The butler came in carrying a lamp with a white fluted globe. He carefully turned up the wick.

"You can pull the curtains now," said Lady Dashbury.

"Yes, m'lady."

The curtain rings were pulled and the candles in the sconces lit by a footman with a taper. While this was going on, the family drank their tea, demolished the bread and butter and made inroads on the cakes, sparing no glance for the intermittent sparkle of gilding on the walls of the ornamental *boiserie* or on the china vases and figures on the mantelpiece as the room glowed with soft light.

Lady Dashbury was frowning and fidgeting a little. She was fashionably dressed with her hair elaborately arranged. Her long white fingers were crowded with fine rings. Beside her sat her sister-in-law, who wore a solid stuff suit with palely striped shirt. Her hair was uncompromisingly scraped back from her brow and drawn into a small bun at the back of her head. The bun was composed of tightly plaited hair fastened into a net. She was sitting munching the good things on the table with the steadiness of a horse cropping grass, taking up each piece of bread and butter with care in large hands with clean square-cut finger-nails.

"It's a pity Cousin Jane wasn't well enough to come down today," said the girl.

"Yes, it is," replied Louise, and again conversation languished.

The family were in their wintry mood, when going out of doors was undertaken for a measure of fresh air, or a landowner's work, or a charitable errand. None of these activities provided food for conversation, only for an occasional comment. This broke a silence which would otherwise have

8

been unbroken but for the faint crepitation of the fire and the clatter of people eating tea.

A diversion came when the door in the middle of the saloon opened and a footman appeared with a silver salver on which lay some letters. He approached Lady Dashbury, who took three letters from the top of the pile, glancing as she did so at the echelon of other letters on the tray. The butler handed her a thin dagger-like paper-knife with which she slit the top of one of her three envelopes, extracted the letter and laid the others down beside her on the table.

"Ludovic wishes to come for a fortnight," she said.

A ripple of interest went round the table. Lady Dashbury said nothing but a faint smile played round her mouth. Lucy looked at her cousin, she was obviously interested.

"Is he coming over from Italy?"

"Ah yes, Italy," Ada said. She compressed her lips and shook her head slightly.

"Shall you let him come, Louise?" she asked.

"I shall certainly let him come; Hugh wishes it," said Lady Dashbury. She had folded his letter up, replaced it in the envelope and slit open another one. Ada said nothing but fluttered the pages of an austere-looking pamphlet, which was all that the post had brought her.

Lucy had received no letters. She was looking at the curtained windows. She had looked up quickly when Ludovic's name was mentioned. Now her thoughts obviously dwelt on something pleasant.

"Lucy," said Ada, "you ought to go up to my mother."

Lucy jumped to her feet, looking a little confused.

"Cousin Jane told me not to come till six," she said and glanced at the ornate ormulu clock whose hand pointed at twenty minutes to six.

"Well then, please go up to my room and find me that paper about the village nurse."

9

As she left the room Ada remarked, "Lucy is always dreaming; she must learn not to waste time."

"No, certainly not," said Lady Dashbury, but it was obvious that her mind was elsewhere.

She rose, remarking, "Hugh is coming back tomorrow afternoon."

"Is Ludovic coming with him?"

"No, he wants to come on Friday."

"Does Hugh want to see Ludovic?"

Lady Dashbury looked sharply at her sister-in-law.

"Ludovic and Hugh get on perfectly well, Ada," she said.

"But I thought that Hugh did not approve . . ."

Lady Dashbury cut her short by repeating, "Hugh particularly wishes to see him."

At that moment Lucy came into the room carrying a letter.

"Thank you, dear," said Ada, "now run along to my mother."

2

LUCY did not exactly run upstairs to see her cousin Jane Dashbury, but she made haste and lost no time. The finely balanced staircase swung a little under her feet as she mounted its shallow steps. She made her way into the gallery which ran round the great hall, and rose from the bottom to the top of the house. The walls of the gallery were adorned by painted Roman figures and trophies of arms, and the gilt balustrades afforded a barrier which nervous people found inadequate as they took an alarmed glance at the black and white marble squares of the floor of the hall far beneath them.

Lucy, who once in her childhood had run breathlessly round the whole length of this gallery, walked calmly along one side into a dimly lit passage and knocked at a door. A quiet "Come in" was said, and Lucy entered, shutting the door softly behind her.

Jane, the Dowager Lady Dashbury, lay on a *chaise-longue* near the fire. She was covered by a white Cashmere shawl. Her high fourposter bed was one side of her and beside it was a Bible and a pile of books limply bound. A glass of water in which stood a sprig of scented geranium was on a table by the bed; another glass with a sheet of paper laid over the top stood beside it.

The face on the pillow, framed by soft smooth grey curls, looked colourless against the fine linen pillow. The pale pink shawl fastened at the throat by a cameo brooch and the blue-veined hands encased in mittens showed under the green-shaded lamp beside Lady Dashbury.

A piled-up log fire burned in the shining steel grate and the room was hot and a little airless. The squat figure of her maid who was bending over her straightened itself up.

"There's Miss Lucy now."

Jane Dashbury smiled. "Come in, dear child," she said, "we shall have a nice time for reading."

The maid handed Lucy a book.

"Well, my dear child, what have you done today?" The voice was surprisingly firm and clear.

Lucy recited her day's doings. They mostly consisted of errands for other people. She had written some notes for Louise and walked through the park with a message for Mundell at the kitchen garden.

"He was rather cross," she added. "Then Aunt Ada wanted some wool wound for the sale." Lucy paused.

"Just an ordinary sort of day," said her cousin." Let's read, Lucy."

Lucy opened *David Copperfield*, and for an hour she and her cousin were rapt away into another world.

At the end of the hour the door opened and the maid came in. "Time for Miss Lucy to dress," she said, "the dressing gong's just going."

Lucy rose and closed the book obediently.

Lady Dashbury smiled at them both. "Can't you give us another five minutes, Soey?" she said.

"You're tired, m'lady, and her ladyship doesn't like Miss Lucy to be late."

"No, I expect you had better go, Lucy. It's been so nice, such an interesting chapter, put the marker into the book and we will go on tomorrow."

Soey brought a small basin of hot water, a sponge and flannel to her mistress's side. Presently there was a discreet tap on the door, a tray was received by Soey, and Lady Dashbury braced herself to eat a small meal for which she had little inclination.

Soey was a nickname bestowed on Mrs. Soames many years ago by one of the family children. Her fellow servants called her Mrs. Soames, although no Mr. Soames had ever lived or breathed. Soey had come to Dashbury Park at the age of fifteen from an orphanage in which the Dashbury family took an interest, and had worked her way up to the august position she now held. She inhabited a pleasant bedroom of her own where she entertained visiting ladies' maids to tea and cakes sent up from the still-room, and where she was waited on by the third housemaid. She had seen the family in all its phases of childhood, youth and middle age. Its drama held her constant interest and attention. The family prestige was something she jealously guarded, and any diminution of it made her unhappy and cross. If any of the family acted out of character, as she in her short range of vision saw it, she showed her displeasure by the tightness of her lips and brief snappishness of her replies. Her heart was given to the Dowager Lady Dashbury, whom she had first seen on her wedding day. She had been allowed to go to the church and wedged into a back pew, not daring to move for fear of a darting glance from one of the upper servants in front of her, and she had made up her mind that some day she would serve the graceful and lovely young bride as her lady's maid.

By dogged hard work and putting her not inconsiderable intelligence into all her tasks, she had risen from fourth housemaid to third, to second, and then when Lady Dashbury's maid fell ill, Soey had been called in to fill her place.

When Lord Dashbury died and his widow moved to the Dower House in the park, Soey went with her, watched over her mistress, and as the years marched steadily on and on, she became more and more a family institution. Her figure was thick and clumsy and her complexion leaden grey, for she had very little contact with fresh air and took no outdoor exercise. The park she rarely visited, and the window from which she looked down on the garden remained mostly unopened. For her it was merely the setting for the gardeners, members of the family or their visitors, who sat on stone seats with lifted parasols guarding their complexions from the sun, or strolled about grasping their long skirts to prevent them trailing on the gravel paths between the low trimmed box hedges in the formal garden.

When this story opens Jane Dashbury had temporarily left the little Dower House in the park as the roof beams in one part of it had shown signs of decay, and she and Soey and a housemaid had gravitated to the big house while repairs were being done. She had been given a bedroom for herself and one for Soey. Her room looked into the branches of an old cedar tree which every year was edging its branches nearer and nearer to one of the windows.

Jane Dashbury missed her own garden. Soey went several days of the week, as she often remarked, to the Dower House to give the workmen a piece of her mind (and Soey's mind when she was bent on an errand of this sort was hardly a present which anyone wished to receive). She was regrettably uninterested in the garden. Had there been anything much to see in it in the winter she would not have noted it, and Jane Dashbury had perforce to be content, when she asked if one of her favourite shrubs had been nipped by frost, with "It looks like a bundle of old sticks to me, m'lady," or alternatively that Mundell, the gardener, had said that if there were no more frosts soon there would be nothing in the garden in the spring, as everything was coming on much too fast. Mundell had sent her some cinerarias and gloxinias. Lady Dashbury was grateful for them, but she much preferred flowers which grew straight out of the earth to the spoiled darlings of the greenhouse.

3

HUGH DASHBURY arrived in the middle of luncheon. He came in and traversed rapidly the distance from the door to the round table at which the family lunched in the long dining-room when there were no guests.

His wife rose to greet him, and he gave her the briefest possible kiss on her cheek, then nodded to his sister and Lucy, seated himself and unfolded his large linen napkin and spread it over his knees.

The three ladies sat more upright in their chairs. Lucy dropped a fork with a mild clatter and her elders looked disapprovingly at her, but Hugh continued his luncheon without a glance in her direction.

"Did you have a good train journey?" asked Louise.

"Quite good," replied her husband, "the train wasn't full."

Luncheon proceeded with its usual ceremony, and at intervals gusts of rain dashed themselves against the tall windows. At the end of it Hugh rose to his feet.

"I am going into the study now," he said, "to look at my letters. I will come and see you in the Red Room in about three-quarters of an hour, Louise."

"Very well," she replied.

He rose and walked quickly to the door by which he had entered.

The three ladies went out at the other door of the long room. Ada and Lucy went upstairs to their rooms, and Louise went into the Red Room and closed the door. She sat down at her ormolu writing table, pulling a sheet of smooth thick writing paper towards her. She dipped her pen into the silver inkstand and wrote a few words. She paused and rested her chin on her hand, staring out of the window, where a light curtain of rain spread itself across the formal garden and the tall trees which bordered the wide green space beyond known as the Valley.

When her husband came in she rose and seated herself by the fire. He sat facing her and pulled some letters from his pocket.

"You've heard from Ludovic?" he asked.

"Yes, he wrote and said that he would like to come this week."

"I saw him in London and he is coming by the four-thirty train."

"I'm glad that Ludovic wants to come and see this place," said Louise.

"Yes, so am I. But I don't know what he will do with himself. I shall take him round the farms; he won't be much interested, but I can't help that. Some of the estate people don't even know him by sight, and that won't do when he comes into this place. Ludovic knows nothing about country life in England, and I can see he cares nothing for it—the duties of a landowner mean nothing to him, he's spent so much time abroad. I shall have to talk to him about business, too. We both dislike that a great deal."

Louise Dashbury looked sympathetic, but in her heart of hearts she thought that for herself it would be agreeable to talk to someone who belonged to the cosmopolitan world which she had once known. She was wearied by talk of pheasant shooting, money or agriculture.

Her husband continued, "I shall take him out shooting too."

"Can he shoot?"

"Well, I understand that he goes after chamois when he stays with those Austrian cousins of his in their castles, but that doesn't mean that he can hit a pheasant coming at him over a covert. However, we shall see. Anyway my mother will be glad to see him." He rose. "I shall go up to see her now. By the way, how is she?"

"Just about the same, I think."

"Have you seen her today?"

His wife put her ringed hand up to her forehead. Hugh glanced at her, she looked a little confused.

"No, not this morning. I sent Lucy up to her while I saw Minchin this morning about the still-room, then I had to go to the laundry."

Hugh made no comment, but she saw that he was not pleased.

"I shall go up now," he said.

As he reached the passage outside his mother's room, Soey emerged from it, shutting the door carefully behind her.

"How is her ladyship?" he asked.

Soey's lips tightened a little. "It's one of her bad days," she said as she moved away from the door. Hugh knocked, and a voice said, "Come in."

He went in and his mother smiled at him. Her face was drawn a little more finely than when he had last seen her. He sat down beside her while they exchanged greetings. He told her a little about the board meetings in London which he had attended. It always came to him with surprise that she showed so much interest in his life in London. She naturally found his banking and business activities hard to grasp, but she listened sympathetically and her eyes brightened when he told her familiar names of men whom he had met at the House of Lords and in his club. These names recalled to her the days when she had been a political hostess. Most of the men Hugh talked about were the sons or nephews of her husband's friends and colleagues.

Presently Hugh took out his solid gold watch and saw that the time was over that he had allotted to himself for visiting his mother. As he rose to his feet he said, "By the way, I had a glimpse of Harriet Warren in London. She is over to consult Sir William Strangways about her boy who is asthmatic. I was walking along Clarges Street past those lodgings where she always stays and she was stepping out of a cab with her little boy."

"How did she look?"

"She looked well and smartened up by Paris, I thought."

"And the little boy?"

"He looks pale but seems very lively. She is staying for two nights at these lodgings where she went as a girl, and then is going to William's aunt Venetia Warren—William cannot leave Paris at the moment."

"Couldn't she come here for a few days, Hugh?"

"Certainly, I will ask Louise to write to her. It would be a good thing for her to be here with Ludovic; it would please him and her to talk about affairs on the Continent."

"I always find Ludovic easy to talk to, Hugh."

"You don't have to talk business to him, my dear mother," said her son. "Well, I shall come and see you again tomorrow."

4

AFTER Hugh had left his mother, she lay even more still than usual with her eyes closed. On her face was a look of someone who was thinking thoughts that were painful. Presently she rang the bell and Soey came in.

She looked sharply at her mistress, opened her mouth to speak and shut it again. There were moments when Soey knew that she must hold her tongue.

Jane Dashbury talked often to her about members of the family, but Hugh Dashbury was never mentioned between them except in passing. He had a sarcastic tongue and could wound and sting his hearers; and in his own home he had that mastery which sprang from being cleverer than his *entourage*. But he attempted no sarcasms with Soey. He would have said, if anyone had thought to ask him, that Soey was too stupid to understand them; but he knew in his heart of hearts that this was not true, and that Soey would clearly understand what he meant to say, and would only show by tightened lips that she liked him less than ever.

Hugh Dashbury had once known a secret garden into which he had entered for a short time. It had been an illicit garden, but it had been full of light and warmth and sparkling joy. Since the gates of it had clanged behind him he had gone on his way without a backward glance. Sometimes he was pricked by a feeling that having been happy with a snatched happiness he should do more to make other people's lives a little pleasanter. He could in fact have set his feet on a road which might have led to green pastures, but in his unhappiness he had descended into an arid desert and there had remained among the dust and stones, wincing at any approach to intimacy and growing year by year a more formidable figure, respected for his ability and hard work but shunned because his tongue had so cutting an edge to it. He had also developed an air of condescension which failed to endear him either to his social equals or to their dependants.

Old Lord Otmoor was heard loudly remarking in his club, "I can't away with Hugh Dashbury, he is so d—d superior. Oh, I know he's clever enough, but I can't stand his airs. He'll have a fine time with his nephew, an odd fish who spends his time in a villa in Italy. Ludovic's father was a nice chap—pity he died, but there's a queer streak there in those Dashburys, a queer streak." Then Lord Otmoor had beckoned to one of the club servants and ordered a fourth brandy and soda after which his hearers heard no more of the Dashbury family.

Years before this story opens and about ten years after his marriage to Louise, Hugh Dashbury had fallen desperately in love with his cousin Dorothy, and she with him. She had been the most admired beauty of her day as a young girl, and many hearts and hands were offered to her, but she refused them all and finally married a distinguished man much older than herself. No scandal had ever touched her name, when one day Hugh and she, meeting at a country-house party, fell in love deeply and desperately. Hugh forgot caution and duty, and the subterfuges to which they were compelled in order to meet did not interfere with his happiness. Dorothy was not only lovely but generous and full of a sort of light-hearted gaiety which he had never met with before. Laughter as well as love had come into his life. Dorothy found that she was going to have a child; they parted and when the child was born it lived for only a few months. She felt that it was a punishment for her infidelity to her husband and refused to see Hugh again. She caught a chill which developed into pneumonia and died a few months after her baby son.

Hugh had deeply wished for a son as he and Louise had no children, their twin sons having died in infancy. He hid his grief under a frigid mask and threw himself into harder and harder work.

Before his affair with Dorothy, Hugh and his wife had gone along together with a fair measure of contentment. Louise had all the attributes which the world imagined her husband would require. She had brought money and a landed property in the north of England to him. She had a sort of cold beauty of face and a manner which concealed her thoughts to perfection.

The affair with Dorothy, of which her friends had told her in veiled terms, had made her feel humiliated and furious. She dared not vent her anger on Hugh or give herself the satisfaction of scolding and forgiving him, for in her heart of hearts she was afraid of him, but her outlook became a little warped and she gained all that she wanted by means which were not always straightforward.

She would not have called herself unhappy. Her social

position was unassailable and as *châtelaine* of Dashbury Park she dispensed charity and patronage. She liked wearing important-looking clothes and fine jewellery. In the world in which she moved she was a woman to be reckoned with socially, buttressed by relationships, money and tradition. She appeared satisfied by her life, and as she possessed no gift for intimacy, the men and women who came to her house never got to know her any better. Her servants approached her warily. Her decisions were capricious and her methods of getting her own way tortuous.

Her husband was aware of this, but he knew that if he said clearly what he wanted done and stated it in brusque terms to Louise, she always deferred to his opinion. But the carrying out of his wishes varied according to her mood, and although she made no open opposition to any course of action he suggested, he was sometimes aware that in small and subtle ways everything had worked out differently than he had planned.

This particular week he had nothing special to impart to Louise; his mind was fixed on his nephew's visit and he had no time to think of anything else.

5

ON Friday the Dashbury family was sitting again around the tea table. The damask curtains were drawn and Louise was wielding the massive silver teapot as usual, and as usual Ada and Lucy were sitting in silence. Hugh with a slight frown on his forehead cut himself a slice of teacake called Sally Lunn and ate it slowly. The room seemed unaware of its inmates. The painted gods and goddesses disported themselves overhead and the brown *boiserie* on the walls glowed darkly except where the gold outlining the panels sparkled as it caught the lamplight. Hugh took out his watch, snapped it open and shut it again without comment.

Then there was a sound outside of steps approaching and the double doors were opened by Bourton, the butler.

"Mr. Taynton, your ladyship," and Ludovic Taynton walked into the room. He went straight over to Louise and shook hands with her, then turned to his uncle, who gave him a handshake so brief as to seem perfunctory, with a muttered "How are you, Ludovic?"

Then he walked round the table to Ada, who rose and shook hands, and then on to Lucy, who gave him a shy smile.

"Sit beside me," said Louise.

Ludovic subsided into a chair beside his aunt and looked all round him with a lively curiosity. Louise asked him about his train journey and he politely gave her his attention saying that he had had an almost empty carriage, the only other inmate being an old gentleman who grunted behind his newspaper.

"Was it Bernard Wilson Fyfield?" asked Louise. "He is a neighbour of ours."

"Yes," said Ludovic carelessly, "I think that was the name on the label of his gun case."

His eyes were still on the room, then his glance fell on Lucy, who coloured and looked down at her plate.

"Ludovic," said Louise, recalling his attention to her.

Hugh rose. "I'm going to my study," he said.

"Can I go and see Grandmamma?" enquired Ludovic.

"Of course," said his uncle. "Lucy will take you up to her room."

The two young people left the room together. When

Ludovic had closed the drawing-room door behind them and they stood together in the dimly lit hall, Ludovic said: "I must have a look at the pagodas."

He walked to where a marble-topped table stood flanked by two Chinese pagodas in tapering glass cases which glimmered white in the dimly lit hall. They were miniature temples where little coloured figures were grouped, bent upon some mysterious pursuit.

"How I loved these as a child," he said. "I couldn't be torn away from them. I was very small, but I admired them even then. Do you like them?" he asked her.

"Yes, I do," said Lucy soberly, "but there's so much to see here and I don't have much time to look at things."

Ludovic followed her silently after that, making no comment. When they reached the gallery of the hall Ludovic said, "How long has Grandmamma been here?"

Lucy turned her head. "About two months," she said. "She's staying till the Dower House is ready again."

Lucy's knock brought Soey to the door.

"Mr. Ludovic, m'lady," she said, as she opened it.

"Ludovic," said his grandmother, "my dear boy, I am glad to see you. Don't run away, Lucy."

"I think Aunt Ada wants me," said Lucy.

"Not for five minutes," said her cousin. "Sit down on the end of the sofa."

Ludovic and his grandmother looked at each other. She had a faint flush on her cheeks. There was a certain likeness between them. Jane Dashbury's soft grey hair had once been as fair as Ludovic's; her aquiline nose recalled his, and if a young unlined face could be said to resemble a face which is drawn in the lines of age and pain, Ludovic and his grandmother were unmistakable near of kin.

"I last saw you at the Dower House," he said. "When are you going back there?"

"I don't quite know," replied his grandmother. "Soey keeps on scolding the workmen, but they only get on slowly all the same."

"Soey looks just the same."

"She *is* just the same," said his grandmother with a smile.

"I was terrified of her," said Ludovic. "When I used to stay at the Dower House she seemed like one of the dragons I had in my fairy book."

"Poor Soey, she isn't really a dragon, she does so much for me and bullies me for my good."

"Poor Grandmamma, I expect you often wish she wouldn't."

"I think I must go," said Lucy. "Aunt Ada wants me to address some envelopes."

"Very well, my dear, run along."

"I have never seen Lucy before," said Ludovic. "She's a remote cousin of ours, isn't she?"

"Yes, her father was Frederic Taynton, a clergyman, and got all his money affairs into a most dreadful muddle. Her mother died and Lucy kept house for him and was wonderfully good and economical, but there was very little left at his death. I persuaded Hugh and Louise to have her here, and both Louise and Ada find her very helpful. She is such a good girl, so unselfish and kind. Now, Ludovic, tell me about yourself."

The next hour passed very pleasantly. Ludovic sat back in his chair, his legs crossed and with his hands clasping his knees.

"So like his father," thought his grandmother with a pang of mixed pain and pleasure.

Ludovic described his life at the Italian villa and his life in Rome where he was an Honorary Attaché at the British Embassy. He had been bred in the diplomatic tradition as his father Richard Taynton had been a diplomat, and had purchased an Italian villa for the times when he was on leave. Ludovic's mother had been half Austrian, half English, but she had never cared for England or for her husband's relations. She was extremely polite to them, but also extremely evasive where they were concerned, and she much preferred a cosmopolitan society to its English variant.

Ludovic's father died in St. Petersburg of pneumonia and his widow settled in Italy, where she died several years later. When it became clear that Ludovic was his uncle's eventual heir, Hugh had to contend for the first time in his life with a variety of annoyances. The first was when his brother Richard's child had been christened Ludovic. It was true that his second name was Hugh, but he was always called Ludovic, and although the boy went to Eton and Oxford, he spent all his holidays abroad in either Austria or Italy and, when he grew up, had been more often in Vienna than he had been in London.

"Shocking upbringing for an Englishman, can't think what Richard's thinking of," was the comment of the Taynton family.

Ludovic as a boy and a youth had dreaded his uncle's visits to his school and college. His uncle managed to import an atmosphere of disapproval into their meetings. His only grudging reference to Ludovic's mother annoyed the boy, as did his uncle's glance at the portrait of her which hung on his wall. She was looking charming, dressed for a Court ball in Vienna.

Hugh had a solid respect for money, but he was not specially pleased when, after Ludovic's mother's death and the estate was settled, it was found that Ludovic, though not rich, was well provided with money, and that the boy was therefore independent of his uncle's control. Another annoying circumstance to Hugh was that Ludovic, after a

25

good deal of idleness at Eton, had worked hard (if unobtrusively) at Oxford and had been awarded a First in Greats.

Hugh did not admire learning as such. He thought it the province of scholars, who earned a meagre living poring over heavy volumes when not engaged in instructing the young. But there was no denying the fact that some people considered University distinction something to be proud of, though it ranked low in the minds of many others. In some circles it was a thing not to be mentioned; the owner of academic knowledge should not be ranked as one of those who carried on the business of the world in a properly serious way.

Jane Dashbury's face had a faint flush and her eyes were bright when Soey knocked at the door at the side of the room and came in.

Ludovic looked at her. "I suppose I must go," he said.

"I'm not really tired, Soey," said Jane, "but," and she glanced at the clock on the mantelpiece, "I expect you had better go, Ludovic. It will soon be time to dress for dinner. Come and see me as often as you wish."

"I will indeed," said Ludovic warmly.

6

DINNER went forward with a certain solemnity. Louise had selected from her wardrobe a purple dress trimmed with velvet. The Dashbury pearls adorned a throat which was still round and white, and her tapering fingers were heavily ringed, her wrists clasped round with heavy bracelets.

Ada's dress was of a nondescript blue, and Lucy wore a black gown as the mourning for her father was still not over.

The candlesticks on the table, the silver sconces on the walls, gave just enough illumination, but the dining-room was shadowed and mysterious. Ludovic exerted himself to talk to his aunt Louise. Hugh addressed a few remarks to Ada, then glanced at Lucy and asked her what she had been doing all day. She was shyly looking at Ludovic, and started when Hugh spoke to her. She coloured with embarrassment and then answered his question in a breathless voice.

When they went into the drawing-room, a whist table had been put out; four silver candlesticks stood on its baize surface, with a large silver matchbox by the unlit candles.

"Do you play, Ludovic?" asked his aunt.

"No, I fear that I don't."

"Well, we'll play dummy whist," said Hugh.

He lit the four candles and seated himself at the table. "You and Lucy can play cribbage."

Lucy indicated a small table near the whist players.

"This is a better one," said Ludovic. It was in fact no different from the other table, but it was further into the recesses of the drawing-room. Lucy fetched the cribbage board and they sat down on each side of it. Unconsciously Lucy lowered her voice as she dealt out the cards slowly.

"I'm afraid I'm not very good at games." She looked up and her eyes met Ludovic's.

"She's got nice brown eyes," he thought.

Ludovic looked round him at the long room and at his elders apparently absorbed in their game. Neither Louise nor Ada was a good player so that playing with Hugh demanded all the concentration they could give, and the murmur of Ludovic and Lucy's conversation hardly reached them.

Lucy found that her alarming cousin laughed easily, made mistakes and didn't appear to mind making them. They plodded along for a little while with their game, and then Ludovic swept the cribbage board over to one side and said, "Let's talk. How long have you lived here?"

"Since last September."

Ludovic was on the point of asking her if she liked Dashbury but thought better of it and absently shuffled the cards. Then he began to lay out a Patience while Lucy watched his long slim hands. He handled the cards neatly and as he bent his head a lock of fair hair fell over his forehead and was pushed impatiently back. She glanced down at his breast pocket where a fine linen handkerchief peeped out embroidered with a monogram, an intricate L H T—somehow it looked foreign.

"I'm not looking forward to tomorrow," he said in a low rapid tone.

"Why not?" said Lucy.

"I've got to have a talk to Uncle Hugh. I shall have to give my mind to business and be disapproved of if I can't understand it."

He swept up all the cards and started laying them out again. Lucy was silent, she well knew that Uncle Hugh's disapproval was not to be lightly regarded.

Ludovic was frowning as he placed a red knave on to a black queen. Then he looked at her. "I'm on the way to being—well, not exactly the family black sheep, but a grey sheep, let us say. I don't fit in with the rest of the flock."

"Oh, I'm sure," said Lucy, distressed at even this mild description of Ludovic's status, "everyone is so pleased that you have come."

28

Ludovic shook his head. "Not Aunt Ada," he whispered, "she regards me . . ."

He did not finish the sentence and went on with the Patience in silence.

The snap of Lord Dashbury's watch was heard in the stillness of the room. He rose and so did his wife and sister.

"Who won the game?" asked Louise.

"Lucy did," said Ludovic, "then I showed her a Patience."

Lucy gave a little start. She had not won the cribbage game, they had abandoned it, and the Patience was one that she knew how to play much better than Ludovic.

The ladies filed out of the room and were each handed a silver candlestick. They said goodnight to Louise and progressed up two staircases to the top floor of the house. Ada said goodnight in a brief tone and shut her bedroom door with decision.

Lucy thankfully entered her little bedroom. It was cold and the fire was almost out, but she was accustomed to this.

Downstairs Hugh said to Ludovic, "Goodnight, my boy, I shall expect you in my study at ten-thirty."

Ludovic went up to his bedroom, chose a French novel from the books he had brought with him, and read till sleep came.

7

THE next morning at breakfast Ludovic looked out of the windows. Rain was splashing down on to the stone urns on the terrace. They were brimming over with water which ran down their sides.

Before breakfast the whole household had attended family prayers in the hall. The servants sat on chairs round a blank space in the middle of the hall. They were all there, the cook, kitchenmaids, housemaids, the butler and footmen and still-room maids.

Ada, her lips soundlessly moving through the prayers and the psalm, knelt beside Louise with Lucy next to her.

Ludovic had the uncomfortable feeling that the household was paying no attention to the prayers and psalms, but that he was being weighed up and compared with his father by the older servants, peeped at by the younger ones. His own frame of mind when the servants trooped out was anything but religious, and he wondered crossly if all this praying did anyone any good at all.

The family seemed untroubled by any doubts and only to have been made hungry by their prayers. Ada had laid her prayer book bristling with bookmarks by her plate. Louise's handsome prayer book bound in purple reposed on a chair beside her. Lucy sat quietly and in silence. Hugh propped the newspaper in front of him and no one seemed to think of disturbing him by conversation.

Presently he rose abruptly and pushed his chair back. "See you at ten-thirty," he said over his shoulder to Ludovic as he marched from the room.

As Ludovic walked across the hall he paused to glance at the pagodas. The little men in blue and red held his gaze for a minute. Then he turned away to pause in front of a monumental square writing table upon whose circumference stood books of reference, including a stout Peerage, a pair of brass scales and a worn leather blotting book with writing materials beside it.

Ludovic walked on, turned the handle of a door, and found himself facing his uncle. The room was darkened by being set inside part of the Palladian portico in the front of

30

the house and also not made lighter by the driving rain outside, and though a large fire burned dully in the grate, the room felt chill and dreary.

Hugh was sitting at a writing table dipping his pen into an inkstand of horn and silver, made from the hoof of a favourite hunter. When Ludovic entered the room Hugh gave him a brief nod, finished his letter, blotted it carefully, addressed it and tossed it into a flat basket beside him.

"Sit down," he said. Ludovic sat down and crossed his legs, and uncle and nephew regarded each other. Hugh locked his hands together in front of him and leaned forward.

"Well now, Ludovic, it's time we had a serious talk. You are coming into this place after my death and you must . . ."

"But, Uncle Hugh, you are not going to die for a long time . . ."

"I hope not, but I am not young any longer and we must face facts; if anything happens to me you will inherit all this."

He looked over his shoulder out of the window to the rain-soaked park. "And you must understand more about it all. You know nothing about English country life or landowning. Your upbringing . . ."—Ludovic frowned and sat up straight in his chair—"well, it's no good going into that now. Landowning can't be learnt in a day, farming's a life's work. Grainger deals with the farmers, and he's a good land agent, but he's leaving and I'm getting a new man. I don't believe in being in anybody's hands however good they are at their work. Grainger I think is entirely trustworthy; he works very hard, but all the same one has to keep an eye on things. The new man is his nephew, and he will take some time to get into the work."

"Do the people like him? Grainger, I mean."

His uncle looked surprised. "I really don't know," he

said. "He's always dealing with grievances, roofs which leak, fences broken down by cattle, field drainage, all that sort of thing. He brings me a lot of complaints, but he puts things fairly to me. No agent is popular unless he gives in all along the line—but popularity isn't everything. I've never bothered about it myself."

"I am sure you haven't," said Ludovic.

Hugh glanced sharply at him. Was the boy being impertinent? But Ludovic's face showed nothing.

"Well, we had better begin. When your grandfather died this estate was very much encumbered. The seventies were very bad years for farming and there had been waste and muddle. I didn't like doing it, but after consulting your father, we sold some land and rounded off the estate to make it more compact. I had been working in London at banking, and I kept on with that and gradually I pulled things round. At the moment things are going better, but it's hard work and needs ceaseless care and vigilance. If your father had lived I should have suggested his coming to live here, but," he paused, "well, it wouldn't have worked."

Ludovic's face hardened at this oblique reference to his mother.

"We must make the best of things now."

Hugh walked across the room to a pile of leather boxes stacked in a corner.

"Open the door, Ludovic, and give me a hand with these."

Ludovic obeyed and they entered a long room with pillars supporting the roof at the far end. Books, calf-bound and impressive, rose in serried rows almost to the ceiling. They looked untouched and unread.

Ludovic carried some of the leather boxes into the library.

"Put them on the floor, please. Here are the keys."

When Ludovic was left alone he took a box at random in

the centre of which was stamped the letter D surmounted by a coronet. The papers inside were neatly stacked and tied together with pink tape. Ludovic stared at them and then cast a longing look round the library. He would so much have preferred to take down some of the books than to bury himself in musty-looking documents. Frowning slightly he addressed himself to his task.

Much later in the morning his uncle found him looking closely at old title deeds going back over several hundred years of Dashbury ownership, with glimpses of stories embodied in marriage contracts and inheritances, with curious old nomenclature of swamp, arable lands and woodlands.

Hugh glanced at the documents that surrounded Ludovic on the writing table. He frowned.

"There's no need to spend a great deal of time on these," he said, "there are many more important things that you must look through. These will do any time, they are all old history and don't concern us at the moment."

Ludovic asked his uncle to tell him a little more about the books in the library. He met with little response from Hugh, who, looking preoccupied, replied that some were considered valuable and that there was a short catalogue of them which only included those on one side of the room. He swept the library with his glance, obviously feeling that as part of the family possessions he should know more about them.

Then he said, "Lucy comes in and makes a list of the books in her spare time." He added, "Lucy is bookish, I'm told, and I said she could do this. Ada doesn't approve and she thinks that many of the books are unsuitable for a young girl to look at. Of course her father allowed her to browse in his library after his wife died; she had no mother to look after her and he brought her up rather like a boy. However I have decided that I shall allow Lucy to do this work of making a list as she won't have time to look at more than the title page of each volume."

"I didn't know Lucy was bookish," said Ludovic to himself. "I must try and talk to her."

The weather cleared next day after a sharp frost in the night. An early morning mist hung over the park, then dispersed and let the sun come through, and Ludovic slipped out into a morning of sunshine. He stood on the terrace above the formal garden and looked across the curving green of the shallow valley. The woodlands which enclosed it on each side stood completely still, unstirred by wind, their top branches delicately outlined against the pale blue sky. Frost sparkled on the blades of grass and made a white covering on the ice of the fountain in the centre of the garden.

Ludovic drew a long breath of icy freshness. He looked back at the house which stood stately and symmetrical, casting a long shadow to the side of him.

The young man was enamoured of the glowing beauty of Italy, but he could not help but feel that here was also beauty of a grave northern kind. He had at moments, through a veil of homesickness, seen the charm of Eton; later he had loved and admired Oxford, in spite of damp, mist and rain. He frowned and went into the house. He did not particularly want to find England beautiful at that moment.

He went into the library through the french windows, hoping not to attract his uncle's attention. Hugh had left the door of his study ajar and had gone out soon after Ludovic came in. Ludovic shut it softly, and took down a heavy tome and became absorbed in its contents. Then he took down another and another book. The sound of an outer door closing recalled him to his task with the papers, and when Hugh looked in he found Ludovic frowning over some legal documents. Asked by his uncle how he was getting on he replied truthfully, "Not very fast. I think lawyers just try and hide the sense of what they mean."

"You will find it easier when we come on to the estate accounts. I'm not asking you to do what I didn't do myself, and if I could do it you can. After all, my boy, you must know how to work—you worked at Oxford."

"I suppose I did," said Ludovic.

His uncle left the room, shutting the door.

"Beastly things," said his nephew resentfully. "I don't believe all this is necessary. Bob Gresham does nothing but hunt and shoot since he came into his place, and he's very popular with everyone."

Then he shook his head hopelessly, he knew that his uncle was talking sense. Ludovic had learnt at Oxford to recognise sense when he met with it. He would, however, have liked to tell Hugh that his studies there, although arduous, had always led him on from interest to interest, while looking through estate documents in leather boxes went deeply against the grain of his mind.

Boredom hovered over Ludovic's head like a raven preparing to pounce. He disliked routine though he was capable of long spells of work. He enjoyed conversation and discussion, and neither seemed to have any place in the life of Dashbury.

When Hugh was absent from the drawing-room, Louise

35

asked Ludovic questions about his life abroad, questions edged with a slight malice. Ada remained silent when this happened and he soon noticed that when any topic did not please her her right foot tapped restlessly on the floor. He saw this first when he was describing to Louise the visit of a Roman Catholic bishop to one of his relations; and when he followed it up with an account of High Mass with its gorgeous ritual in a Cathedral she murmured audibly "Popish practices," and left the room.

As she reached the door she said to Lucy over her shoulder, "Come along, you must help me finish those lists." Lucy rose reluctantly as she had been listening to Ludovic with close attention and interest.

Louise, whose hands were occupied with some fine white embroidery, replaced her needle in an emery cushion shaped like a small strawberry. She looked at Ludovic and leant forward and said, "Now tell me about your mother's half-brother, Count Rudolf, and that Viennese singer."

Ludovic was a little taken aback, but he repeated some of the better-known gossip about the famous soprano at the Opera. It sounded flat in his ears and a little stupid, but his aunt drank it in with eager interest. Soon the clock on the mantelpiece struck six with silvery precision.

He rose. "I must go and see Grandmamma now," he said.

Louise looked disappointed; she wanted to hear so much more. But she took up her needle again, merely remarking, "Yes, do go."

When Ludovic reached his grandmother's door it was opened as usual by Soey. She drew back as he went in, he kissed Jane Dashbury's cheek and she patted his shoulder.

"What's happened to Lucy?" he asked.

"I've let her off her readings to me at this hour. She goes to her room and reads to herself."

"I never see Lucy in the day-time. We talk a little after dinner but we can't raise our voices for fear of disturbing the whist game."

His grandmother smiled. "I am sure you will like her," she said. "She is very shy and reserved and difficult to know but well worth knowing."

"She is always running errands for Aunt Louise or Aunt Ada and being sent post haste out to the gardens with messages, or addressing envelopes for Aunt Ada, or making lists of something." Jane Dashbury sighed. "Why in the world does Aunt Ada want all this done?"

"Well, Ada does work hard, she has always thrown herself into work for other people." Jane paused and went on, "When she was a girl she was in love with a cousin of yours but he went away without asking her to marry him. She became very silent and I tried to take her out of herself but she wouldn't talk to people or make friends. Then one day she told her father that she wanted to go as a missionary to China; but he would not hear of it and she stayed with us as the daughter at home, and when Hugh succeeded he asked her to stay on in this house. She comes to see me at the Dower House when I am there, every day. I sometimes think that my husband did wrong not letting her be a missionary. I should have urged him to consent but it seemed so far away in those days. It was impossible to think of one of our family doing such a thing."

Ludovic was silent; he too found it hard to think of such a thing. He also found it difficult to imagine Aunt Ada, so precise in her ways, confronting, Bible in hand, a mob of pig-tailed Chinese, facing danger, perhaps . . .

There was a silence. Jane Dashbury seemed lost in troubled thoughts, then her face cleared a little.

"You must tell me more about yourself," she said. "When one is old and not well one tends to brood too much on the past and to see too clearly how people should have acted or should not, and to be powerless to help them to change, ah me . . ."

"Don't they take your advice, Grannie?" he asked.

She smiled. "I don't believe in giving advice," she said. "People don't alter their ways because they are advised to do so by an old woman who lives out of the world. Soey is always hinting that things might be done very differently here, but she knows it is no good. I won't even try to interfere."

9

THE following day Louise retired to bed with a cold. The myriad draughts and cold blasts of air in the icy hinterland of each room, out of reach of the large fires which burned in all the grates, made the Dashbury inhabitants very susceptible to coughs and bronchitis during the winter.

At luncheon Ada said that she wanted some things bought in Dashbury. "You can go in the pony cart, Lucy," she said.

Hugh stared. "Nonsense, my dear Ada, it's much too cold for the pony cart. Lucy can have the brougham."

Ada pursed her lips. "But, Hugh, Marston was out for a long time yesterday."

Hugh cut her short. "It won't hurt him to go out again today, and the horses need exercise."

"Can I go too?" said Ludovic. "I should like to take a look at Dashbury while Lucy does Aunt Ada's errands."

"Very well," said Hugh, "you can go if you like." He

said over his shoulder to Bourton, "Tell Marston to be round with the brougham in half an hour, to take Miss Lucy into Dashbury. He can put up at the Dashbury Arms till Miss Lucy is ready to come back."

He added to Ludovic, "Yes, you can take a look round Dashbury. I can give you an errand to do at Thomas the saddler's. Marston will tell you where to go. There isn't a great deal to see but you should know your way about there."

After luncheon Ada drew a list from her black reticule.

"Come and talk to me, Lucy," she said, and she drew Lucy aside into the embrasure of one of the long windows in the drawing-room, and the two men heard murmurs of "Don't forget—please try and match it exactly—you know last time . . . I'd like to come myself but I promised to go and see Mrs. Robson."

"I'll try and manage," said Lucy, looking confused.

Bourton's voice cut across the talk in the room. "The brougham is at the door, m'lord."

"Off you go," said Hugh. "Get your hat on quick, Lucy, don't keep the horses waiting."

"Goodbye," said Ada, "and don't forget the red flannel."

"We might be leaving to go half across Europe for all the fuss she makes," thought Ludovic crossly as he left the room.

The brougham moved off smartly and Lucy with the rug tucked round her knees, and clasping her shabby reticule with her gloved hands, stole a look at Ludovic.

He was looking frowningly out of the window, then he sighed. "Well we've got away for a little while," he said. "How thankful I am."

"Oh, Ludovic, don't you like being here?" said Lucy in a distressed voice.

"No, I don't," he said, "it's such a strain," he burst out.

"Aunt Louise and Aunt Ada don't seem to get on, and Uncle Hugh does nothing but tell me the dullest and most tedious things. I'm only happy when I'm with Grannie. She looks as if a puff of wind would blow her away—but she's a dear, and interesting and sympathetic, and wants to hear about other things than this great place and the little tedious things about it."

Lucy was silent, it voiced so much of what was in her own mind. Tears often came unbidden into her eyes as she thought of her life with her father. Their casual meals eaten at times which suited his parish work, their reading aloud in the evenings, their joint enjoyment of books. Then of the services in the little church so poorly attended for lack of parishioners in the small village where they lived, and her father's sermons when he strove to conceal his erudition and make them plain for everyone to understand.

There she had been Miss Lucy, the Vicar's daughter, with her recognised position in the eyes of all the grown-up inhabitants of the village, who had known her since she was two years old. At Dashbury Park she was a poor relation, taken in from kindness. She sighed in her turn.

"They mean to be kind," she said. "I am sure they do."

"Made you into an unpaid drudge," muttered Ludovic. He seemed relieved by his outburst and Lucy noticed that they were coming into the outskirts of Dashbury. A farm-house stood beside a cluster of farm buildings with grey roofs and walls stark against colourless fields and dark woods frozen into silence. Then came some small houses, then rows of even smaller ones, then a market square. Marston turned the horses under an archway into a court-yard where a gnarled and twisted wistaria, flowerless and leafless, clung to the low buildings surrounding the court-yard.

Ludovic shivered, it looked so shut in and cold. He

helped Lucy out of the brougham, then their ways diverged as they emerged from the archway and Ludovic set out to find the saddler's.

The market place was empty of passers-by. Ludovic walked quickly and saw the name Septimus Thomas written in brown letters on a white ground above a door. He bowed his head as he went through the low doorway into the little shop. An old man was sitting polishing a piece of leather. He peered sideways at his visitor through steel-rimmed spectacles.

Ludovic explained his errand and laid the girths and stirrups he had brought on to a wooden bench.

"Would you be Mr. Taynton?" the old man said. "Mr. Ludovic?"

Ludovic nodded.

"I knew your father well, Mr. Richard that was. I am glad to see you, sir. Mr. Richard he used often to come in here and see me when he was a lad. Fine rider he was, good hands and a good seat on a horse before he went so much to furrin parts—a pity he died. Yes, well . . . I knew his old lordship and her ladyship. How is her ladyship?"

"She looks frail but says she is well," replied Ludovic.

The old man shook his head. "She's had her share of trouble she has. After Mr. Richard died she came in here looking like a ghost of herself. Always came in to see me, she did, tears in her eyes when she spoke of him. Yes, she's had her share of troubles same as we all have—and his lordship, is he well?"

"Very well," said Ludovic, who had never given the matter a moment's thought.

"Works hard in Lunnon he does, not like most squires round here, but he gets his bit of sport, too. He's working to help keep the place up, I reckon. Will you be here for a while?"

"Yes, for a little while."

"Going back to furrin parts?"

"Yes, I have work in Rome."

"Dear, dear," said the old man, shaking his head.

When Ludovic emerged at last from the dark little shop he made his way to the church, which stood at an angle of the market place.

10

LUDOVIC crossed the market square diagonally. Two women conversing in a doorway stared at him and he heard an upper window flung open. He quickened his pace and passed under a lychgate into the churchyard. A Norman tower stood up four-square against the cold sky. Between him and the church were gravestones of many different shapes and sizes, and to his left the spreading blackness of an ancient yew tree. On a solitary stone under its dry shade his eye was caught by his own name. 'Maria Taynton, died 1793, aged twenty-two. Beloved by all who knew her, her sorrowing family erected this stone to her memory', was inscribed on the tombstone.

He stopped and stared. Poor Maria, he mused, wondering why her life had been so brief, and how much her family had really sorrowed for her. Maria lay there under the dark spreading branches forgotten and solitary in her death. He shivered a little and quickened his pace to the church door and pushed it open.

He had half-unconsciously expected it to be like an

Italian church, scented with faded incense and mouldering in a sort of sunny decay. Though he was nominally a Protestant and had attended Chapel at Eton and his College Chapel at Oxford, Ludovic was always slightly repelled by the cold neatness of the church of his forebears. In this church at Dashbury he seemed unable to get away from his family. He inspected the tombs in the chancel where Sir Hugh de Ashbury, who fell in the Crusades, lay with some animal, dog or lion, at his feet. Opposite was another figure in an Elizabethan ruff, the name anglicised to Sir John Dashbury. Then his eye travelled upwards. He saw a classical-looking tablet inscribed with the name of the first Lord Dashbury ennobled by William Pitt, then looked to the window above the altar into which the glass with its bright yellows, blues and reds had obviously been inserted at no distant date. The garish colours made a jarring note in the quiet old church.

He left the church casting only a side glance at Maria Taynton's tomb, and walked rapidly across the square regardless of the intent gaze of two men who stopped unloading barrels from a brewer's dray to gape at him. He quickened his pace and passed through the archway into the inn courtyard. Marston and the ostler were harnessing the horses and Lucy, looking quiet and withdrawn, was standing in a doorway.

"So sorry to keep you waiting," said Ludovic.

"I have only just come," she replied.

They mounted the steps into the carriage and turned into the square. Marston touched the horses lightly with his whip and they started off at a quick pace. Ludovic did not look out of the window till they were on the road leading out of Dashbury.

"Did you get all your errands done?" he asked.

"I think so," said Lucy frowning and looking downcast,

43

"but I couldn't get enough red flannel or quite match the buttons. I'm afraid Aunt Ada won't be pleased."

"Well, it's not your fault if you couldn't get them."

"No," said Lucy, "it isn't exactly my fault, but Aunt Ada may think it is. She . . ."

"Why, what would she have done?"

"She would have made them have everything out of the drawers and cupboards in the shop on to the counter, but somehow I couldn't ask Mrs. Cooper to do that, she looked ill and her husband is bedridden. Did you go into the church?"

"Yes, I did. I first of all saw a Taynton grave under a yew tree."

"Oh yes, Maria Taynton, she died of a broken heart when her young man jilted her."

"Then I went into the church. It seemed full of our tombs and tablets, and there was a very brightly coloured window put up to Grandpapa. Then I came away. Do you go to church there much?"

"We are supposed to go there once or twice a month, but we also go to Belling near the Dower House. That's where your father is buried," Lucy said a little breathlessly. She went on, "Cousin Jane wouldn't let him be buried in Dashbury; she said his grave must be near, so that she could take flowers herself and put them on it every week. Before she got ill she used to go there a lot, but now of course she can't go, and you see Mr. James at Dashbury is High Church and Mr. Gibson at Belling is Low Church."

"I see you can take your choice. Which do you like?"

Lucy sighed. "I don't like either very much," she said, "but I have to go when I am taken. My father's services weren't either High or Low, he said that country people only liked a plain reverend service."

"What does Uncle Hugh like?"

44

"He only goes to church occasionally and mostly to Belling, but sometimes he goes to Dashbury and sits in the family pew; Aunt Louise is High Church and Aunt Ada very Low. Aunt Louise has a mother-of-pearl crucifix in her bedroom."

Ludovic was silent. He had heard echoes of religious controversy in Oxford, but the set of young men to which he belonged were interested in other matters and theological controversy was apt to be dubbed as tedious.

"Does anybody mind," he said, "I mean about her having a crucifix in her bedroom?"

"Aunt Ada doesn't like it at all; she turns her eyes away from it every time she goes in there."

"Why shouldn't Aunt Louise have it," said Ludovic, "if she wants to?"

"I don't know, but it seems to matter very much here."

At that moment the carriage passed under the porch of Dashbury Park, the horses' hoofs made a hollow clatter which reverberated to the roof.

11

LADY HARRIET WARREN* had been invited to come to Dashbury.

"When is Harriet coming?" asked Hugh.

"She wants to come at once for two nights—bringing little Charles with her," replied Louise.

* Her adventures are told in Susan Tweedsmuir's earlier novel *Cousin Harriet.*

"Surely a very short visit."

"Yes, but she cannot leave William's Aunt Venetia for longer—William has probably told her that she mustn't leave his aunt for long, he tells her what to do," said Louise blandly.

"Harriet strikes me as having a mind of her own," said Hugh.

"Yes," said Ludovic. "I have heard a lot about Lady Harriet. She is much liked in diplomatic circles and praised for her tact and charm. Sir William is spoken of as one of our best diplomats: she is a great help to him."

Louise was silent.

"Well, I shall be glad to see her here," said Hugh. "I was entertained by them in Paris, and I am glad to make some return for their hospitality."

That evening when Ludovic visited his grandmother he asked her about Harriet.

"She is only a connexion of ours, not really a relation, but she is charming, I believe. The Waveneys have always had charm. They are a quiet family and before Harriet married she lived down at Waveney with her father, who died two or three years ago. She met her husband, who was then at the Embassy at Rome, through her cousin Victoria. I have never heard anything but good of her."

"Grandmamma," said Ludovic after a pause, "do you think that Uncle Hugh would let me ask my Oxford tutor here for a day or two? I know he would like to see the library."

His grandmother smiled at him. "Tell me about him, what is his name?"

"He's called George Maxwell. He is Scotch and his subject is the seventeenth century, and I have looked at some books of that date in the library. I like looking at books of that date myself, but I haven't George's knowledge or scholarship, and anyway I never get a chance of handling

46

them as Uncle Hugh always takes me away to look at dull papers, or to talk to me about business."

His grandmother's eyes rested a little anxiously on Ludovic's face. "Well, my dear, there is a lot you will have to know when you come into this place."

Ludovic made an irritable movement. His grandmother made no comment; instead she enquired, "What is your Mr. Maxwell like?"

Ludovic considered for a moment. "He was very kind to me when I was up at Oxford and we used to go for country walks and talk a lot. He is shy but very interesting when you can get him to talk."

"He is Scotch you said?"

"Yes, his father is an impoverished Scotch laird in the same sort of country as Sir Walter Scott's Abbotsford. It is pretty country, he says, not high mountains but endless green hills. George seems very fond of it, he walks a lot and knows it well."

"Green hills," said his grandmother softly. "I've sometimes wished we could see green hills in the distance here. But this is nice country in its own way, and one can't have everything," she sighed. "I should like to walk on grass again. I used to walk so often in the park and through the woods."

Ludovic received a slight shock; he had forgotten that he had seen her walk when he was a child, and now thought of her only as immovable in shawls.

Jane Dashbury smiled at him. "Yes," she said, "that's all long past for me. Well, Ludovic, you want Mr. Maxwell asked here?"

"Yes, it's term time now, so that he couldn't come for more than a Saturday to Monday, but perhaps he might come again if Uncle Hugh liked him. Could you ask him, Grandmamma?"

"Are you so shy of your Uncle Hugh that you can't ask him yourself?"

"He's a difficult person to explain things to," said Ludovic, frowning. "He's so preoccupied and brusque and I don't believe he likes having people to stay."

His grandmother gave a light little sigh. "Louise likes it," she said, "he lets her have large parties in the summer, but he is sometimes difficult about having people here at this time of year. The men shoot and hunt of course and Louise has to entertain their wives; if it pours with rain that isn't easy, and then Hugh finds the evenings very long. But anyhow, your Mr. Maxwell can always entertain himself in the library—yes, Ludovic, I will ask your uncle about this."

She did so and Hugh agreed to it after some demur. She had reminded him that Ludovic was young and should be ridden on a light rein.

"Well, I hope he hasn't got it into his head that the library is what interests him most; he's not easy to talk to about estate business."

"He doesn't find you easy either," thought Jane, but she did not voice her thoughts.

Ludovic went to see Louise. She was seated at her writing table frowning a little.

"But, Ludovic, I don't know what to say to an Oxford don, they talk above one's head all the time."

"George Maxwell wouldn't do that, Aunt Louise. To start with he talks very little himself."

"But that makes it more difficult."

"Not really, I don't think, he's such a good listener. Anyway, he'll be in the library most of the time; you won't see him except at meals, and he's only here for two nights."

"Very well, I will write to him," said Louise, heaving a sigh.

Later in the day Ada said across the tea table, "I hear that you want to have your Oxford tutor to stay, Ludovic. Is he interested in Foreign Missions?"

Ludovic blinked a little. "I've never heard him speak of them," he said cautiously, but added, "Do ask him, Aunt Ada. Oxford is always interested in outside things."

"Missions are not outside things," said Ada, drawing back in her chair and planting her feet firmly on a footstool. "We should all try to do our duty by the heathen."

"What exactly is our duty to them?"

"That they should be converted and made to wear proper clothes and not to practise witchcraft."

Louise rose from her seat at the tea table suppressing a yawn. "We will wait tea for Harriet," she said, "who will be here any minute."

'I am beginning to wish that I had never suggested George coming here', thought Ludovic.

12

HARRIET WARREN entered, leading her little boy Charles by the hand. The whole party rose to greet her. Louise and Harriet were on terms of formality. She had never seen Ada or Lucy, so they met with handshakes instead of embraces. Harriet's face lit up when she saw Ludovic. Then she glanced nervously at Charles. She guided his small hand into each outstretched hand as he disliked polite greetings only a little less than he did being kissed by unknown (or known) ladies. Free to look round him he gazed upward at the gods and goddesses on the ceiling.

"Messenger is waiting for him outside," said Harriet. "I'll take him to find her," said Ludovic.

Charles followed the tall young man into the hall which was dimly lit and mysterious.

Soey was standing by Mrs. Messenger and they were conversing in low tones. Charles hardly glanced at them, but looked round him and his glance alighted on the pagodas which flanked the marble table. He darted forward, pressing himself as near as possible to their stands and peering through the glass case, his dark eyes alight with pleasure and excitement.

"What are the little people doing?" he asked.

"They are in some sort of temple in China," said Ludovic.

Messenger advanced. "Now come along, Master Charles, say how do you do to Mrs. Soames, there's a good boy."

She grasped Charles' hand and he was led away between the dark squat figures, his head turned back over his shoulder to look at the enchantment he had just discovered.

Harriet's eyes had followed Charles' small figure out of the room. She was anxiously hoping that he would behave properly. She had not wished to bring him to Dashbury, but her husband's aunt, Venetia Warren, had developed a very bad cold and Charles caught cold easily and had a tendency to asthma. William Warren had suggested in a letter Harriet's staying at Dashbury, where he had been as a boy.

"I hear that old Lady Dashbury is very ill," he said. "I know she would like to see you and I should like you to tell her how well I remember her kindness to me. Louise Dashbury will be polite to you; she is only rude to people who are strangers to her own world, and anyway, my dearest, it is only for two nights. I wish I could be with you."

Harriet after reading the letter arranged to go to Dashbury, but as she looked round the company at the tea table her heart sank a little, and she wondered how she would get through the next two days. When she turned to address a question to Ludovic the eyes of the company were upon her. Louise seemed unaware of Ludovic's quick response to Harriet, Ada's bustling curiosity, or of Lucy's eyes open wide with interest.

When tea was over, Harriet asked if she could go and see Charles and then Jane Dashbury.

"Yes, Lucy will take you up." Lucy jumped quickly to her feet.

Harriet's bedroom was large; even the massive and petticoated dressing table and the fourposter bed seemed dwarfed by its size. The door near the fireplace was ajar and through it came the sound of a childish voice high pitched in argument.

Charles was standing by a hip bath wearing an air of impatience. Messenger was kneeling beside him enveloped in a large apron. On seeing Harriet Charles cried out, his words tumbling over each other.

"Mamma, Mamma, have you seen those little Chinese men standing talking to each other under a lot of roofs?"

Harriet wrinkled her brow and put her hand on to Charles' forehead; an anxious look came into her face.

"I think he means the pagodas in the hall," said Lucy.

Harriet's face cleared. She had thought for a moment that Charles' babble betokened a temperature.

"Mamma, if I walked about this house alone should I get lost in these passages?"

"Come to bed," said Messenger, "you won't get lost if you don't go prying into things which don't concern you."

Harriet bent over her son who rose with a quick movement from saying his prayers. They were an almost unintelligible gabble and his mother had had to prompt him

51

several times, as his mind was obviously not on his devotions.

As her bedroom door closed Harriet said to Lucy, "Charles is so excitable, and we have a time of it keeping him quiet. Helen, our little girl, is as round as a ball and never gets into a temper; everyone calls her Mother Bunch."

Harriet took up a miniature from a table and Lucy saw a child clasping a doll, smiling and curly headed.

There was a knock on the door and Louise stood in the doorway. "I hope Charles is all right?"

"Thank you, I think he will soon be asleep."

"Will you come and see my mother-in-law now?"

Louise's long skirts brushed softly against the thick carpet in the passages. She carried herself as if she was entering a state ball and Harriet felt impelled to be silent. Soey admitted them to Jane Dashbury's room.

"I have brought Harriet to see you."

Soey had draped her mistress with her best shawls. The *jardinière* was filled with fresh hothouse flowers and the fire blazed brightly in the steel grate. Jane Dashbury lay on the *chaise-longue*, a faint colour in her cheeks.

"It is a pleasure to see you," she said.

13

THE following morning Lucy offered to take Charles for a walk in the garden. They went out of the front of the house into a frosty windless morning. Charles threw a stick for Jester, Louise's stout elderly terrier, and then looked up into Lucy's face while he chattered to her. They walked round the house and passed through a small ornamental iron gate and went down some stone steps to where Neptune, slimy with green water weed, and with inflated cheeks, for ever blew a soundless tune on a conch shell. Charles stood by the low stone coping surrounding the fountain, which was not playing as it was frost-bound.

Charles stamped his foot on the ice in a puddle with the gratifying result that a small white star appeared on the dark brown surface of the ice. He did it to another frozen puddle while Lucy stood smiling beside him, duly admiring his prowess, and then taking his hand she urged him forward into the garden for fear that by standing still he should catch cold.

She herself drew in a long breath of winter air and thought how pleasant it was to be out with a child and to listen to his chatter, which flowed on like a shallow brook with no hidden depths, twists or corners.

"There's Miss Lucy out with Master Charles," said Soey, opening Lady Dashbury's window a crack and peering through it. She quickly shut it again. Fresh air was Soey's enemy with which she fought on the whole a winning battle, as far as her own and her mistress's rooms were concerned.

When Harriet brought Charles into Jane Dashbury's room later in the day he came in dragging at her hand with obvious reluctance. Lady Dashbury showed no surprise at his unwilling handshake, but opened a heart-shaped silver box at her side, and with an apologetic lift of the eyebrow to Harriet, offered him the box. Charles sat down near his mother, his eyes roving round the room, his eager questioning sealed by the large sweetmeat in his mouth.

"I can hardly keep Charles away from the pagodas," said Harriet.

"Yes, they are a world within a world and children always like a miniature of grown-up life."

They talked for a few minutes and Jane Dashbury enquired, "Have you seen anything of Lucy, Harriet?"

"Not so far, she usually comes into a room and is out of it again before I can say a word to her."

The two sharp vertical lines on Jane's forehead deepened a little. "Yes, I fear that Lucy isn't given much time for conversation. She should have more than she has. And what do you make of Ludovic?"

"I like him," said Harriet, "and I know that William thinks him very clever."

"I fear he is not at ease here."

Jane took up a little handbell from the table beside her and Soey appeared.

"Take Master Charles into the gallery, Soey, please, and show him some of the house for about half an hour, and then bring him back here."

Soey grasped Charles' hand after he had accepted another sugar plum. When they had left the room Jane said:

"I hope you don't mind, but it's better to talk when there are no small ears pricked to listen. I am disturbed about Ludovic. As I was saying, he is not at ease here."

"With you he seems to be."

"Thank you, Harriet, but he and Hugh are not happy together; he comes into the title and this place and Hugh naturally wants him to understand something of the estate and the working of it all. Hugh isn't old but life is an uncertain thing and accidents do happen. Hugh is not hunting this season because he strained his arm, but he will certainly go back to it and he rides very hard—but I suppose one mustn't see dangers ahead."

There was a moment's pause, then she continued, "I always thought that my son Richard, Ludovic's father, loved Dashbury, but his wife wished him to live abroad and he only came here to see me. I pinned my hopes on Ludovic. Now I feel that this whole place bores and oppresses him."

Harriet was silent, and all at once Soey came in with Charles, who ran towards his mother crying, "Mamma, I've seen the Chinese men."

Soey looked severe. "Nothing," she said, "would serve Master Charles but to go and see those things in the glass cases, he wouldn't so much as look at anything else."

"He has never seen anything Chinese before," said Harriet apologetically.

Jane smiled indulgently. "Children always love them," she said. "Look, Charles, I think I have got a little Chinese man, and I will give him to you as a present before you go away."

That evening Harriet sat at the massive table in her bedroom writing to her husband.

"Here I am at Dashbury, and oh, my dearest, I feel so lost without you. They are kind here, which makes me feel ungrateful, not that I think they particularly like me, I just think they are being good-mannered to me. Louise asks after you quite a bit, Ada remembers you as a boy, but I can't make any headway with either of them, they keep me at arm's length. Ludovic Taynton is here, he would be amusing but he looks cross and at odds with everything. Louise is avid of gossip about Paris and *how* I dislike this. She presses me with questions about the Embassy and the people we know and although I know you sometimes smile at my extreme discretion, I know you really approve of it. Ludovic began by egging her on, then quickly (and he is very quick) gave a twist to the conversation and told some amusing anecdotes about Rome. A young Taynton cousin is living here called Lucy. She is very silent and shy and seems to do nothing except run messages and do things for the family all day long. So far I have hardly had a chance of a word with her but Charles has taken to her. The one person who is kind and sympathetic is the Dowager. She must have been lovely in her youth and she still is charming to look at, wrapped up in shawls on her sofa. She asked a great deal about you and then talked about Ludovic; apparently there is friction between him and Hugh as he is the heir and he seems bored by all the business of his future inheritance. Charles is very happy, he is in love with the Chinese pagodas in the hall. I am terrified that he will damage one of their tall glass cases (I am sure they would break at a touch and if he is not prevented he *will* try to lean against them to peer inside). The tables in the drawing-room are strewn with valuable objects which he might over-turn. I shall be thankful to get back to Aunt Venetia. Ludovic's Oxford tutor, a Mr. Maxwell, is coming this afternoon. I wonder if the place will seem rather oppressive after the austerity of an Oxford College.

Your own Harriet.

P.S.—I don't think that Dashbury is as beautiful as Waveney. You will smile when you read this as you always say that in my estimation no house can compare with our own home.

14

GEORGE MAXWELL arrived at teatime—Hugh was coming by a later train. Announced by Bourton, George walked into the room his head erect. He looked remote and a little forbidding as he advanced towards Louise without glancing at the rest of the company.

Ludovic stood aside while the introductions were in progress. He smiled at George, who remained imperturbably grave, and sat down beside Louise, next to Ada.

'Poor old George,' Ludovic thought to himself, 'this is going to be a great ordeal for him, he does look *farouche*.'

He addressed himself to lightening the atmosphere and trying to find some topic which would set the conversation going. He could think of nothing except to enquire about George's journey. "I'm afraid it must have been long and cold."

"I am well used to cold," said George Maxwell. "Trains in Scotland freeze continually."

George looked gravely round the table, till his eyes met Lucy's, who looked down at her teacup. Then he turned to Louise, who was looking at him with scarcely veiled surprise. She had listened without interest to Ludovic's remarks to Hugh about his Oxford tutor, and if she gave the subject any thought at all it was to imagine George Maxwell to be an elderly gentleman with a white beard and a bald head and a scholar's stoop. This young man (George had just turned thirty) with his erect carriage, thin face and alert eyes, was something quite new and unexpected.

'Dear me,' thought Ludovic, 'George never had any small talk. I *must* get the conversation going somehow.'

"Have you ever been in this neighbourhood before?" he asked.

"Never," said George. "I have been on walking tours from Oxford, but not in this direction."

"I expect that you find England very different from Scotland," said Ada.

"George misses his mountains," said Ludovic, "the Oxford country is so flat."

57

George looked at him. "There are no high mountains in my part of Scotland," he said, "only one or two biggish hills."

At that moment the door opened and Harriet came in. "I do apologise for being late," she said, "but I was reading aloud to Charles and I didn't realise how the time was going until Messenger came in to say that tea was ready."

Harriet was not being strictly truthful in her excuse. While she read aloud in her bedroom, Charles had leaned over the writing table and had seized and tilted the inkpot at a dangerous angle. The ink had poured out and Harriet had been mopping it up with all the available blotting paper in her leather blotting book. She had left Messenger to try to eradicate the stains finally. She had descended the stairs thanking her stars that she and Charles were leaving on the following day.

Harriet looked across the tea table at Ludovic, who cocked an eyebrow at her with comic despair. She quickly took charge of the conversation, and addressing George directly, recalled a visit which she and Sir William had paid to the head of an Oxford college and described the Encænia ceremony. Gradually the atmosphere lightened. George smiled, and Harriet managed to make Louise and Ada at least give a fair show of interest in what was being said.

When Hugh arrived the ladies had dispersed to their bedrooms, and he found George and Ludovic talking together in a small room reserved for smokers. After shaking hands he took up a stand in front of the fire, silently looking down into the flames. His days in London had been heavy ones, the train slow and the carriage cold and yet stuffy, and he was not in the mood for conversation.

Ludovic saw this, and rising to his feet, knocked out the ashes of his pipe saying, "I will take George up to his room, Uncle Hugh."

They mounted the curving staircase which swung a little under their feet. George looked up on the panelled walls to the two Venetian lanthorns on either side of the stairs, in each of which a small lamp burned with a steady flame. Separated by a passage at the head of the stairs the gallery round the top of the hall stood in faintly illuminated darkness seen through an open door.

Lucy came through it carrying in her arms a pile of paper-wrapped books. She paused when she saw the two men.

"What *are* you doing?" said Ludovic.

"I'm taking these books down to the hall for Aunt Ada. They've got to go off early in the morning."

Ludovic was struck by a sudden thought. After a moment's silence he said, "The Aunts have gone up to their rooms and Uncle Hugh into the study, let's go downstairs and talk a little."

Lucy looked doubtfully at him.

"Come along," said Ludovic, and he turned and walked down the stairs. In the drawing-room he motioned Lucy to an armchair by the fire and he and George seated themselves.

"Now, Lucy," said Ludovic, "you've looked at the books in the library."

"Oh, only a few, Uncle Hugh asked me to make a list."

George looked at her with surprise. "Are you a student of the seventeenth century, Miss Lucy?"

Lucy looked confused. "No, indeed," she said, "I'm not a student of anything; only my father had a lot of old books and Uncle Hugh knew that, and he asked me to take some notes when I had time, that's all."

"Nonsense, Lucy," said Ludovic, "I should call you a bookish person, but I don't suppose you do much reading here?"

"I try to do a little, my father said I should read something every day. He didn't mind my reading novels if they were good ones."

"Which writers do you prefer?" asked George. "I hope you like Sir Walter Scott?"

Lucy's face lit up. "He's my favourite writer," she said.

The discussion which ensued was mainly carried on by Ludovic and George, with Lucy putting in a word here and there. Her face glowed with interest. George told her of a visit to Abbotsford.

"Is it beautiful?" asked Lucy eagerly.

George said not exactly beautiful, more impressive perhaps, but sad, when you think how Sir Walter broke down his health by overwork to keep it going.

"I remember my grandfather telling me that he met the Sheriff, as they called Sir Walter, riding along and he stopped and they had a talk. My grandfather said he had never talked with a pleasanter or kinder man."

"That's just what I should have expected," said Lucy thoughtfully.

"Do you also like Thackeray?" asked George.

"Not quite in the same way," replied Lucy, "but I have *Vanity Fair* always by me, and I've read it many times. But Aunt Ada thinks that reading novels is a waste of time."

George looked astonished. "Does Miss Ada Taynton really think that reading historical novels by great writers is waste of time?" he asked.

"Well, she says that one must never read a novel in the morning, and later in the day it isn't easy to do it."

Ludovic sat listening to this conversation, his eyes travelling from one speaker to the other. He thought of the box of novels and *belles lettres*, French and otherwise, in his bedroom, to which he often had recourse in moments of boredom; and he felt the pang of sympathy (which one reader has for another) when he thought of Lucy's few chances to indulge her passion for reading. He had meant to offer some books to Lucy (not of course French ones, they were unsuitable for the perusal of a young lady), but some others. Well, he would do so in case she had a chance of looking at them.

The boom of the dressing gong reverberated through the hall as Bourton beat a tattoo on its massive bronze surface.

Lucy sprang quickly to her feet. "Oh, dear, I must go," she said as she ran out of the room.

George and Ludovic followed more slowly. "It's a heinous crime to be late for dinner in this house," said Ludovic.

George made no reply to this and they walked upstairs in silence.

After dinner the ladies adjourned to the drawing-room while the gentlemen went into the library. Harriet found herself sustaining the conversation. There seemed to be a paucity of topics and there were disheartening pauses while she tried to think of something to say which might interest both Louise and Ada. 'Surely we have talked of this before, more than once,' thought Harriet. Her head ached, and she glanced surreptitiously at the clock.

Charles had behaved fairly well all day. The pagodas, in spite of his alarming pressure on their glass cases, had remained uninjured, and the ornaments in his mother's bedroom were intact. No more ink had been spilt on the writing table.

Harriet looked at Lucy, who was doing some charitable-looking needlework. Lucy looked up and their eyes met.

'I would like,' thought Harriet, 'to do something for that poor girl. I wonder if perhaps some time she could come to London for a day or two.'

Ludovic came into the room. "Uncle Hugh asked me to say that he has gone to bed. George is in the library absorbed in books, he asks to be excused from coming to say goodnight. He will put out the lamps in the library, and I have given him a candle to light him to bed."

Much later George, to whom time was as nothing when he was studying his favourite subject, made his way through the dark hall, candle in hand. He pursued his way slowly and carefully, found the staircase in a well of darkness, and as he walked up the final steps his candle picked up the gilding on the Venetian lanthorns.

He paused for a moment because into his mind there flashed the vision of a girl coming through the door of the gallery carrying a pile of books, whose brown eyes had met his for a moment when she saw him with Ludovic.

15

HUGH, Ludovic and Lucy stood in the hall when Harriet took her departure. Her presence had lightened the atmosphere of the house and when Hugh shook hands with her he said:

"Come again, Harriet, and bring William with you next time."

Charles had one hand in Harriet's firm grip, and in the other he held a wicker basket which contained a small china figure of a mandarin presented to him the evening before by Jane Dashbury. He went through the ceremony of farewells as perfunctorily as possible when under his mother's eye, then cast one last lingering look at the pagodas as he passed through the front door.

Louise was breakfasting in bed, and Ada after a brief farewell to Harriet had disappeared up to her room.

As the brougham drove off Harriet permitted herself a sigh of relief. On the whole she felt that her visit had gone off well. She was sorry to say goodbye to Lucy and Ludovic, and Hugh in his own way had been nice, but she thought 'I couldn't make any headway with Louise and Ada, but old Lady Dashbury was delightful and George Maxwell interesting. I must try and do something for Lucy.' She checked these thoughts and turned to Mrs. Messenger, who sat beside her.

"Did you enjoy your visit?" she said.

"Yes, m'lady. Mrs. Soames was very nice, she showed me all her ladyship's wardrobe and all the satins and velvets, and Mr. Bourton showed me his plate room and the gold-plate dinner service they've got, and Mrs. Gristwood showed me her kitchen, but it's not as light as the Waveney kitchen, rather a dark place I thought, and then Sarah took me to her linen cupboard. Her ladyship goes in very much for embroidery on the sheets and pillow cases. Sarah had them all out to let me see. The linen at Waveney is getting to such a pitch, m'lady, that, patch as I do when I'm there, it's getting to look very old."

"We must get some more in Paris," said Harriet.

"The Paris shops are not like London, m'lady."

At this moment Charles endeavoured to lean out of the window trying to see a black sheep in a field, thereby endangering his own safety and his mother's flounces. 'Well, anyway,' thought Harriet as she restrained him, 'Charles didn't damage anything much and William will be pleased that I went to Dashbury.'

After Harriet had taken her departure, Hugh with more

politeness than enthusiasm accompanied George Maxwell and Ludovic into the library. Ludovic took down an old leather-bound volume. Hugh made an irritable movement: he had no desire that his nephew should bury himself in a book as he had other plans for him. He turned to Ludovic and said, "Didn't Lucy make a list of some of the books?"

Ludovic replaced the volume. "Yes, I believe she has," he replied. "Shall I go and fetch her?"

"Yes, certainly."

Ludovic knocked on Lucy's door. As he did so, Sarah the head housemaid came along the passage.

"Hullo, Sarah," he said, "I've come with a message from his lordship."

"Miss Lucy's in Miss Ada's room," she said; her look conveyed impatience and compassion.

Ludovic went on down the passage and again knocked at a door.

"Come in," called Ada's incisive voice.

Ludovic had never entered Ada's room before. It was crowded with large pieces of furniture. From the windows he saw a segment of the park which rose in a gentle slope to a belt of aged and knotted oak trees. Ada was sitting at a massive writing table backed against the wall. It had mounting tiers of pigeon holes into which had been thrust bulging envelopes secured by thick elastic bands. Magazines bearing the initials G.F.S. were stacked on the floor. Ada turned her head to look at the intruder, and Lucy, who was kneeling on the floor, looked up in surprise.

"Uncle Hugh wants Lucy to come down to the library."

Lucy dropped the pamphlet she was holding, and the colour rose in her face. Ada looked displeased and her lips contracted.

"Uncle Hugh wants you to help with the books. You made some lists of them, didn't you?"

64

"Well, only two rather short ones," she replied.

"Go along, Lucy, at once," said Ada, "don't keep my brother waiting."

As they progressed downstairs Ludovic remarked, "Aunt Ada seems rather short in the temper this morning."

"Well, she's had rather a difficult letter today from one of her Societies; they don't quite want to do anything she suggests, and she doesn't like me to be taken away. Oh, Ludovic, I don't know if I can be of any help about these books."

"Nonsense," said Ludovic, "of course you will," He seized her hand. "Come along, let's run across the hall, it will help to clear your head."

Ludovic opened the library door.

"Come in, Lucy," said Hugh. "Where are those lists you made?"

"In the writing-table drawer."

Hugh compared his large gold watch with the clock on the mantelpiece. "Now, Ludovic, look sharp. I said we would meet Grainger and his nephew, the new agent, at eleven o'clock."

Lucy had opened the writing-table drawer. George, book in hand, was gravely regarding her.

As Ludovic left the room he was smiling a little to himself.

Lucy shut the drawer and looked up. "I am afraid," she said confusedly, "that I only made a few notes. I started at that corner of the library and dusted some of the books and put them back in a better order—they were all pushed in there anyhow, some back to front. I hope I didn't make a mess of them."

"I am sure that what you did will be of value," said George. He seated himself on the opposite side of the writing table. Lucy's handwriting was clear and well formed. George turned the pages and looked across at her.

"This will be a big help," he said, "there is so much to look at in this library and I cannot give much time to it. Could you show me which is the part of the library you spoke of?"

Lucy showed him and as she took a thick volume a fine cloud of dust spiralled into the air.

"I must go and get a duster," she said.

When she returned George was again studying her notes. "You have unearthed one or two interesting things," he said, "and now can you please show me just where these books are situated?"

He had moved to the corner of the room. A pale ray of sunshine found its way slanting through the window, and as George examined book after book the motes danced in the light. It was impossible not to feel cheerful this morning, thought Lucy, so unlike her usual mornings at Dashbury.

They had got into a sort of rhythm of work, George taking the books out of the shelves and Lucy running the duster round their bindings.

George worked in silence, and as he laid down each book on the table he described it briefly to Lucy. He asked her to give him back a book from the further side of the table. She lifted it with care and came towards him, holding it out. He took it from her, but as he did so it slipped, and in catching it their hands touched. George grasped the book firmly and Lucy turned away and again took up the duster.

"You are not tired, Miss Lucy?"

"Oh no," she said, "this isn't tiring; it's only uninteresting things which are tiring."

"I fear we all have to do uninteresting things at times."

"But surely you do interesting, worthwhile things all the time?" she asked, as she stood looking at him, duster in hand.

66

"Well, I don't know—there are college meetings which drag on and on."

"Yes, they must be tedious but not exactly dull, and your teaching, and working at books . . ."

George regarded her for a moment. The sunshine outside had triumphed: it shone through the winter clouds and came into the room touching Lucy's hair with light.

"But," said George slowly, "you have surely time here to read: the treasures of the mind can be yours. I gather that you do read from our conversation last night."

"Yes, whenever I can."

"Shall I make you a list of books to help you in your reading?"

"I should be grateful," said Lucy. "As you would do for one of your undergraduates."

"I'm sorry if I sounded a bit didactic," said George.

"Please, please," said Lucy, "I didn't mean that; it would help me so much, I am very ignorant."

They resumed their labours in silence and by the end of the morning several shelves were well arranged, and the books, their film of dust removed, shone with Lucy's careful polishing.

George had stacked some books on the writing table. They were of special interest to him.

"I will speak to Lord Dashbury about them, and put your list back in the drawer."

Hugh and Ludovic came in. Behind his uncle's back Ludovic put on a pantomime of extreme exhaustion, and Lucy was hard put to it not to laugh, but George went on arranging his notes.

"Did you have a pleasant morning?" asked Louise at luncheon.

"I worked away," said George, "and I had very good help from Miss Lucy."

The two ladies said nothing.

"How are you getting on?" asked Hugh politely.

"I have only touched the fringe of the library," said George. "I have found some very interesting stuff. I will put together what I have found for you to see."

"Yes, please do," said Hugh. "By the way, there is a little book written by an aunt of mine, have you got it somewhere, Louise? I daresay it doesn't give a very accurate account of the family—ladies don't go in much for accuracy, but it might give you some idea of our family history."

This somewhat sweeping assertion about ladies caused no comment from Ada and Louise, and George, who knew several eminent lady scholars at Oxford, should have taken up the challenge. But after looking round briefly at his companions at the table, he did not feel it worth while to say anything. His eyes met Lucy's and he felt her disappointment that he did not take up the cudgels for her sex. He opened his mouth to speak, but at that moment Louise rose from the table and the opportunity was lost.

"Come along, Lucy, I will give you Aunt Selina's book and you can take it to the library."

"Then please come up and see me; I want you to go along to the Vicarage with a basket," said Ada.

A quarter of an hour later Lucy came in and handed George a small vellum-bound book with a coat of arms painted on it. She turned to leave the room.

"Don't run away, Lucy," said Ludovic, "before we've had a look at this."

"Please stay, Miss Lucy," said George.

The book proved to be charming. It was nicely planned. The coat of arms of each lady who had married a Taynton was well emblazoned at the top of a page where any facts known about the said ladies were written out in a careful script. The family portraits had been copied in miniature, and if the drawings were a little vague and unprecise, they had caught something of the interest of the originals. The whole book had the attraction and interest of a labour of love.

"Aunt Selina lived here a great deal, didn't she?" said Ludovic.

"Yes, here and at the Dower House all her life," Lucy replied.

"Do you mean that she never went away?"

"Only once a year for a fortnight to the sea."

"Good heavens," said Ludovic, "poor thing: how dismal for her. Fancy . . ."

"She might have lived in far worse circumstances," said George. There was a tinge of reproof in his voice. "She might have been brought up in a slum dwelling, or in a manufacturing town. Here she had leisure and fine surroundings."

Ludovic shrugged his shoulders and George continued to turn over the pages of the little book.

Ludovic took up a book from the writing table and began to read.

The door closed quietly and the two men looking up saw that Lucy had disappeared.

"What do you think of this library?" asked Ludovic.

George raised his head, and pointed to some of the bookshelves. "I would say that that part of it is an eighteenth-century gentleman's library bought in bulk by the first Lord Dashbury. It is a handsome collection, very representative of its kind, but there is nothing much in my line of interest there. But the earlier books are extremely interesting and, I should say, valuable."

"I had no idea that anyone in my family had ever had any interest in collecting books at all," said Ludovic, putting the book he had taken up back on to the table with a slam. "Nowadays Aunt Louise never opens any book except an insipid novel, and Uncle Hugh never reads anything but the newspapers. Aunt Ada reads nothing but pamphlets and tracts—but my grandmother, I must say, does read a lot. She's nice to talk to about books."

"My father and mother do not read," said George, "but that hasn't prevented me from reading and studying. People in Scotland respect study and learning."

"Well, they don't here," said Ludovic crossly.

On the first evening of his visit to Dashbury George had admitted that he played whist. He proved to be an exceedingly good player, but the second evening he begged to be excused and to go and continue his work in the library.

Lucy and Ludovic, each with a pack of patience cards in front of them, started laying one card upon another. Suddenly Ludovic said, "Let's go and see what George is doing." He rose quickly, nearly overturning the table.

The three elders turned their heads to look at him.

"What are you doing?" asked Ada.

"We're going to see if we can give George a hand with the books."

"There is no need for Lucy to go," said Ada. "There's some needlework over there . . ."

"Oh, go along, both of you, do," said Hugh, frowning and annoyed at being disturbed in his game. He was holding good cards and foresaw an easy victory.

When they reached the hall Ludovic whispered, "That was a near thing; come along quick."

The fire in the library had been made up and the lamps glowed with a soft light through fluted paper shades. Above the marble mantelpiece hung a picture in which some mysterious figures pursued their avocations in what appeared to be a landscape with trees, mountains and a river. The mantelpiece was flanked by two marble busts. In front of the fire two armchairs with tables, a lamp burning on each one, suggested leisured study.

'This could be a nice room,' thought Ludovic, 'if someone who liked books ever sat here.' He started to imagine himself doing this, then shook his head and stood staring in front of him.

16

GEORGE had been ushered in by Soey to Jane Dash-bury's bedroom. For a moment he thought of his own grandmother as he stood on the threshold of the bedroom, and the warmth and the scent of flowers surprised him. Invalids in Scotch country houses received short shrift in the matter of warmth and flowers; they usually sat bolt upright in bed in useful flannel nightgowns with dark brown woollen shawls round their shoulders. The softness of the atmosphere and the pale pink design on the embroidered white shawl covering Jane's small nearly recumbent form, pointed a luxury he had never known or envisaged.

His own grandmother had strongly marked features. She held all countries outside Scotland (with the possible exception of France because of the 'auld alliance') in deepest contempt. Her father had lived in the troubled days of the '45, and his tales of those times had filled her with a resentment against England which the passage of years had done little to soften. She used to sit in a corner of their drawing-room knitting, straight-backed and stone deaf, more a revered institution in George's family than a pleasant companion.

When George had decided to try his fortune in the green pastures of England she had raised every possible objection. He found that no description of the architectural beauties of Oxford or of its fame as an institution of learning moved her from her stern disapproval of the place. In one respect, however, she did smile slightly when he spoke of Oxford. It might be a good thing for this place set in lush meadows by sluggish streams to have a Scotchman there. He could assist in the affairs of an effete southern university and in their teaching of young men, and she understood that there were other men in Oxford who came from Scotland, and who presumably would see that justice was done to the Scotch undergraduates who, mistakenly, as she thought, sought to be educated there.

While these thoughts flickered through George's mind, he stood looking at Jane Dashbury, and when he came out of his momentary abstraction, he met a pair of blue eyes full of an intelligent alertness.

She started the conversation by saying that she had once met Doctor Jowett, and that one of her husband's contemporaries had been head of an Oxford college. From this she went on to ask him about his researches amongst the books at Dashbury.

"I've browsed so often in the library," she said, with a note of sadness in her voice, "but there never seemed to be much time, and my husband was always so much occupied with politics and money matters. The late seventies were such bad years for agriculture, and anyhow he was not a man for books, nor indeed is my son Hugh. But Richard," she added, "Ludovic's father, loved books and collected them and Ludovic has the nucleus of a fine library at his villa in Italy." She shifted her position a little restlessly on the sofa. "How do you find Ludovic, Mr. Maxwell?"

"He is shaping well; his mind is a good one, and though he does not say anything about it, he has great powers of work. He is a good talker, and an excellent listener."

"You don't think that he is irresponsible? I mean afraid of responsibility?"

"Few young men welcome responsibility except those who are too old for their years, and they are apt to develop into pompous prigs in later life."

"I fear he does not care for the thought of coming into this place."

George was silent. He had heard much from Ludovic on this subject, and his native caution made him chary of expressing an opinion.

At that moment there was a soft knock on the door and Lucy entered the room. "Oh, I'm so sorry," she said when she saw George. "I'll come back."

"No, come in, my child," said Jane. "Lucy always reads me *David Copperfield* for an hour, and we both enjoy it. We won't read this evening, however. Lucy, sit down on the end of my sofa."

Lucy obeyed, clasping the book. George was considering her with grave attention. He was glad that she had come, as he had no wish to be questioned about Ludovic's plans or ideas. She sat very quietly looking at Jane Dashbury, then turned her head and their eyes met. He found himself staring at her and roused himself to hear what Jane was saying.

"Lucy and I read mostly Dickens or Thackeray. Have you any other books you can recommend to us for reading aloud?"

George thought for a moment. "There is a Mr. Robert Louis Stevenson, an Edinburgh man, who has written some

73

interesting essays and some stories which carry one along. He has a great gift of narrative."

"Lucy, please get me my little ivory notebook, it's over there somewhere, and write down the name of this author and his books."

Lucy fetched the book and spread the tiny ivory leaves out like a fan. She found one on which nothing was written, and wrote busily at George's dictation.

That evening, after George had said his goodbyes to the family, Ludovic and he repaired to the library.

"Your uncle has asked me to return here in April."

"Can you manage it?"

"Yes, I can spare a few days after the University goes down."

"Well, Uncle Hugh must have taken to you, he isn't lavish with his invitations. I hope you will come back; I'm afraid you have found my family heavy in hand—some of them at any rate."

George gave Ludovic a glance. He seemed about to say something, but thought better of it.

17

"A NEIGHBOUR of ours, Mrs. Wilson Fyfield, and her stepdaughter are coming to tea today," Louise said to Ludovic several days later. "Will you be back from shooting?"

"Yes, Aunt Louise."

Hugh looked up. "I shall have tea in the library," he said.

"Oh, Hugh."

"Well, I don't care for Theresa Fyfield, and I've got some letters to write."

"Well, what shall I say to her?"

"Don't say anything. She won't want to see me; there's no love lost between us." At this he rapidly drank a cup of tea and left the table.

Louise shrugged her shoulders. "Then I shall count on you, Ludovic, to help."

"In what way?" asked Ludovic. "Is this lady so difficult?"

"She is a vulgar worldly woman," said Ada, as she left the table, and Louise, murmuring something inaudible, walked out of the room.

At five o'clock Bourton announced,

"Mrs. and Miss Wilson Fyfield."

Louise rose gracefully from her armchair by the fire to greet them. She towered over Mrs. Fyfield, who advanced with a gloved hand outstretched. She was followed by her stepdaughter Katharine, who was as tall as Louise and walked forward with girlish awkwardness, looking a little like a young colt who, if approached by strangers, is likely to bolt to the other end of the field. Keeping her eyes on her stepmother's beaded cape, Katharine stumbled over a footstool. Mrs. Wilson Fyfield darted an angry glance at her over her shoulder.

"Oh, I'm sorry," said Louise, "those footstools are always in the way. Put it in a corner of the room, Lucy, please."

Scarlet with embarrassment, Katharine shook hands with Louise, and the greetings over, Louise seated herself behind the tea urn. Katharine sat down next to Lucy.

"I do wish Cousin Harriet was still here," thought Lucy, "she makes talking so easy." She rose to help Louise by distributing the cups.

75

Mrs. Wilson Fyfield's voice had a penetrating quality—none of the present company could fail to be aware of what she said.

'Well, anyway, this girl and I needn't talk,' thought Lucy as she handed the cups round the table.

At that moment Ludovic entered the room.

"He's got that shut-up look on his face," thought Lucy.

Mrs. Wilson Fyfield, who had been describing to Louise a fashionable watering place she had visited, stopped abruptly.

He was introduced and sat down in the vacant place next to her.

Lucy felt Ada's eyes upon her. "She'll ask me afterwards why I was stupid and didn't talk," she thought.

She turned to Katharine and asked how far she lived from Dashbury, noticing as she did so the girl's grey eyes under a broad forehead and her generous mouth.

"I don't quite know," Katharine replied, "we came along a lot of muddy lanes."

Lucy searched her mind for further conversation. "What do you do all the time?" she asked.

"I hunt a lot. Do you hunt?"

Lucy shook her head. "I don't even know how to ride."

"What do you do?"

"Well, sewing, and I help Aunt Ada and Aunt Louise"—she stopped.

Katharine looked as if she would like to hear more, but at that moment they heard Katharine's stepmother say to Louise, "You haven't seen Katharine since she came out?"

Louise looked politely interested and leaned forward and beckoned Katharine to come and speak to her.

Katharine stood up, tall and shy, and then sat down beside Louise.

Lucy moved to another place and Katharine's stepmother sat down beside Ada.

"It's like the Mad Hatter's tea-party in *Alice in Wonderland*," Lucy thought, and from the glint in Ludovic's eye she saw that they shared the same thought.

Louise turned to Katharine and tried to engage her in conversation, Katharine answering in monosyllables.

Louise looked at Ludovic, who in the reshuffle at the table found himself next to Katharine. She asked him if he had seen the new agent.

"What's he like?" she asked.

"He seems quite clever," said Ludovic. "He's much quicker at picking up business things than I am."

"Your Uncle Hugh says that you don't give your mind to business."

Ludovic frowned. "I like business of a kind. I find my work in Rome easy and interesting." He addressed himself to Katharine.

"Have you ever been here before?" he asked.

"Only once, when I was ten," she replied. "I played hide-and-seek and then we went into a sort of Chinese room."

"It's a good house for hide-and-seek," said Ludovic, "endless passages and dark corners."

"Could you show Katharine the Chinese room she remembers?" asked Mrs. Wilson Fyfield. She had to all appearances been talking to Ada, but she now craned her head forward to ask this question.

"Of course," said Ludovic politely. "Come along too, Lucy."

Mrs. Wilson Fyfield darted a glance at the young people. Under the mask of conventional amiability a pucker of annoyance showed round her mouth.

Ludovic led the way into the Chinese room. It looked

shadowy and a little forbidding with its blue vistas of slender odd-shaped trees where small men hunted strange quarries. The lamps were burning dimly.

"Yes, I remember this," said Katharine, in a low voice. What a contrast to her stepmother's loud one, thought Lucy.

Ludovic wandered about the room picking up one small object after another and putting it down again at once.

"Do sit down," said Lucy to Katharine, pushing forward a Chinese Chippendale chair. Katharine sat down with a murmured "Thank you."

"Do you know the history of the things in this room," said Ludovic to Lucy, "to tell our visitor?"

"No, I don't," said Lucy. "Aunt Louise and Aunt Ada don't seem much interested in the history of anything here—I asked about the Chinese things once and they only said that a great uncle of yours had brought them back from China from some palace. I wish I knew more . . ."

"The contents of this house are perhaps more interesting than its inmates," muttered Ludovic.

Lucy had picked up a small leather-covered book from a table and was looking at it. Katharine had heard Ludovic's *sotto voce* remark.

"Yes, I think that's often true," she said.

Ludovic looked at her. "Do you like houses?" he asked.

"Yes, better than people," she replied. "Houses stay still and leave you alone."

Lucy looked up for a moment from her book, then looked down again at its tiny woodcuts. It was only a week since she had been working in the library with George Maxwell.

Ludovic went over to the marble mantelpiece. He flicked the top of one of the pendants of two glass lustres and it swung, making a clicking noise. He leant across the fireplace and flicked its companion ornament with his finger.

"Oh, Ludovic," cried Lucy, "*do* leave those things alone, they break at a touch, and they've only just been mended. I took them to the mender in Dashbury a month ago."

"Oh, don't fuss, Lucy," said Ludovic. "The breakages in this house must be enormous and one or two more won't hurt."

Lucy looked up surprised by his tone. "In that case why add to them?"

Ludovic flung himself into a chair and stared at the lustres. The pendants swung to and fro and gave out faintly disturbed tinkling sounds.

Lucy laid her book down. "Do tell us about your season in London," she said.

Katharine looked down at her hands folded in her lap and then at Lucy. "I went to a lot of balls," she said, "one or two a week, and to the Opera and Ascot, and once or twice to a play."

"The conventional young lady's season," said Ludovic.

Katharine's eyes rested gravely on him for a minute. "Yes, I suppose it was," she said slowly. "I didn't enjoy it much, though the other girls I know said they did; but I am not much good at making conversation, and my step-mother gets cross if I don't talk."

"It's very hard to know what one likes or doesn't like in this world," said Ludovic, with mock sententiousness.

'What's come over Ludovic,' thought Lucy, 'he's being so very tiresome.' Aloud she said, "I've never been to a ball in my life, and I've always wanted to go to one."

"Well, make Aunt Louise give one for you."

At that moment the door opened and from its threshold Bourton announced: "Mrs. Wilson Fyfield's carriage is ready, miss."

Mrs. Wilson Fyfield was saying effusive goodbyes and begging Louise to come over to luncheon. "And do come too, Mr. Ludovic," she said. "I shall call you Ludovic, I think, as I knew your father."

As Katharine and her stepmother drove home, the latter remarked, "I suppose that girl Lucy Taynton is a sort of poor relation. What's she like?"

"Very nice," said Katharine. "I'd like to see her again."

Her stepmother made no answer and there was silence in the carriage as the horses clop-clopped along, the glow from the headlamps illuminating the hedges which bordered the silent fields beyond.

18

A FEW days later when breakfast was over Ludovic crossed the hall. He had read till all hours of the night, and was consequently feeling cross and sleepy. He had not been in time that morning for family prayers. Nothing was said to him by the family, though Ada looked frosty and rubbed her hands together, a trick of hers when she was put out. Ludovic carried off his truancy from prayers as best he could, but it always made a bad start for the day.

He paused this morning to look at the top of the marble table which stood between the pagodas. The day's letters were set out in neat piles, and glancing over them he saw one addressed to Lucy. Beneath it was a package which obviously contained a small book. Ludovic recognised George Maxwell's handwriting. Something prompted him to take the letter and parcel and to stuff them into the capacious pocket of his tweed jacket.

Looking up he saw Ada advancing towards him across the hall. He took up a letter for her and held it out.

"Good morning, Ludovic, I hope you slept well."

"Very well, thank you."

"You had some letters, Ludovic, I saw you stuffing some into your pocket."

Ludovic made no reply, but picked up another letter. "I'll take this up to Grandmamma," he said and left the hall without a word.

"That will teach her to meddle with other people's business, inquisitive old cat." He ran up the staircase two steps at a time and knocked at his grandmother's door. He was admitted by Lucy.

"I have brought you a letter and a parcel," he said, looking at her with a slight smile as he took them out of his pocket. When Lucy saw the Oxford postmark she coloured with surprise. Letters were rarities in her life, in fact she seldom received one.

After greeting his grandmother, Ludovic sat down beside her. "I must go soon," he said, "Uncle Hugh has got Grainger coming and he wants me to talk to him, or rather to listen to what they are saying."

"Shall I come back?" said Lucy, who was sitting by Lady Dashbury.

"Yes do, my dear."

Lucy dropped the book and the letter into her reticule and fled down the passage and up the stairs to her room. She took the stairs to the top floor at a gallop. She saw Ada's retreating back going through a door. The moment it was closed she walked rapidly to her own room, closed the door and opened the letter. It was written on the note-paper of an Oxford College.

"Dear Miss Lucy," it began,

"Following on our conversation at Dashbury I am

sending you a book of Robert Louis Stevenson's essays which I think you might enjoy reading to Lady Dashbury.

"I have a very pleasant recollection of my work in the library at Dashbury Park and of the help you gave me. I look forward to returning there in the spring.

Yours sincerely,
GEORGE MAXWELL."

Lucy unwrapped the book, glanced at its title and then unlocked the drawer of a small escritoire, placed it inside and locked it again. She paused for a moment while the key, which hung on a fine chain round her neck, dropped into the bosom of her dress. Her small serious face was lit up by a look of expectancy as she inwardly promised herself a quiet perusal of what the post had brought her.

She went back to Jane Dashbury. Ludovic had left and Soey was standing talking. Lucy heard her voice:

". . . and you wouldn't believe, m'lady, what those workmen are doing to the cistern, drip, drip, drips going on, ruination of the floor underneath, if you ask me."

Jane Dashbury listened patiently—she looked a little weary. "I'll ask his lordship to send down Jarvis to see what's going on."

Soey looked quietly martyred. "Well, if Mr. Jarvis can make them work, I'm sure I'm very glad. I gave them a bit of the rough side of my tongue." She turned, saw Lucy, and grumbling to herself left the room.

Lucy sat down.

"Will you write a note for me to your Uncle Hugh? I want to ask him if Jarvis can go and take a look at the workmen at the Dower House. It's rather difficult because Soey and he are at daggers drawn, but it has more authority coming from Hugh. Soey scolds the men each time she goes there, and they no longer pay any attention to what she says."

82

Lucy obediently sat down, her thoughts elsewhere. She wrote at Lady Dashbury's dictation. When it was finished Lucy said, "Mr. Maxwell sent me a letter and a book of Robert Louis Stevenson's. He says he thinks I might like to read it aloud to you."

If Jane Dashbury felt any surprise she did not show it, she merely looked interested. "How very nice of him," she said. "I always like reading a new author. When you write and thank Mr. Maxwell, tell him how much I shall enjoy hearing it read and give him my thanks too. Bring the book along this evening."

Lucy's heart beat faster; she had not gone so far as to consider her reply to George Maxwell.

A few days later Louise received a note from Mrs. Wilson Fyfield inviting herself and Hugh, Ludovic and Ada to luncheon. Lucy was not mentioned.

"I don't wish to go," said Ada, and gathering up some printed matter, she left the room.

Ludovic was reading a newspaper.

"Will you come, Ludovic?" said Louise.

"Well, I suppose I must," said Ludovic ungraciously. "Why isn't Lucy asked?"

"I don't know," said Louise.

"Well, I think she should go," said Ludovic. "She never goes anywhere, and if she doesn't go I shan't go either."

Hugh came into the room at that moment, and saw with surprise a frowning Ludovic and a puzzled Louise. Louise explained the letter to Hugh.

"Lucy isn't asked and Ludovic says he won't go if she isn't. Ada isn't going."

Hugh looked impatient. "Well then, when you answer, say that neither Ada nor I can come, but that you are bringing Lucy. Surely that's quite simple. Come along to my room, Ludovic. Don't stand any nonsense from Theresa Fyfield," he said over his shoulder as he left the room.

Louise moved to her writing table and took up her pen, and the letter was duly written and despatched.

Mrs. Wilson Fyfield read Louise's letter. She looked annoyed, for although Hugh and she had cordially disliked each other for many years, she would have liked him to come, and she had purposely not included Lucy.

"Hugh's not coming," she said to her husband.

"Sorry for that. I suppose he's in London."

"Ada isn't coming either."

"Sorry for that too. I rather enjoy a scrap with old Ada, we never agree, but . . ."

"Louise is coming with Ludovic Taynton, and they are bringing a cousin with them whom I did not invite."

The General, who was occupied in feeding his stout and wheezy spaniel, made no reply.

The day came and Louise, Ludovic and Lucy set out. There were foot-warmers at their feet and ample rugs covered their knees. The late February day had borrowed some beauty from a later month of spring. Out of a cloudless sky the sun shone on fields sparkling with frost; the road was iron hard with ruts and puddles covered with thick ice. The horses' hoofs rang loudly as they went at a fast trot. Presently the warmth inside the brougham made a film over the windows. Ludovic took out his handkerchief and polished a section of the window nearest to him.

Louise leaned back in her seat. She disliked going out in the winter and she foresaw no pleasure from the visit. Lucy was silent too and if either of the other occupants of the carriage had been thinking about her they might have noticed that she looked softly happy about something, as if she was thinking pleasant thoughts.

Ludovic stared out of his patch of window. He had often told himself (and others) how much he disliked the sodden darkness of an English winter, and this shimmering sparkling morning raised his spirits. He began to whistle a little snatch of a song sung by fishermen in Italy. They were passing along a ridge of hill crowned by a beechwood, the polished grey stems of which caught the reflection of the sunshine. They turned a corner and saw below them a stream which ran in loops through a water meadow. A long rambling house stood above it.

Louise roused herself, sat bolt upright, adjusted her dress, smoothed down her pale suede gloves.

"Have we arrived?" asked Ludovic.

"Yes, almost," she said, as the carriage swept in between two stone gateposts.

"Open the window please," and as Ludovic did so the keen frosty air came in to dissipate the thick atmosphere inside the carriage.

Under the classic portico of the older part of the house their host and hostess awaited them. Mrs. Fyfield greeted Louise with effusion, shook hands vigorously with Ludovic, and gave Lucy a brief handshake.

The General shook hands with all three guests with equal (or equal lack of) warmth. They were ushered into a room in which a welcome fire blazed steadily. A little sunshine came in through the windows and the scent of greenhouse flowers filled the room. It gave the impression of a heated box not at that moment ungrateful to Lucy, who had only ventured to put her feet on the end of the rapidly cooling foot-warmer in the carriage and whose head from the steamy atmosphere of the brougham was hot in contrast to her feet.

Louise was led to an armchair by the fire and Ludovic was removed by the General to the smoking-room.

85

Katharine came in. She greeted Louise and her face lit up when she saw Lucy.

'She has a nice smile,' thought Lucy.

Louise was shielding her complexion from the fire by a small palm-leaf screen. Her feet reposed on a beaded footstool. Mrs. Wilson Fyfield drew forward a large firescreen made of peacock's feathers. Louise looked round the room, the walls of which were thickly strewn with dark portraits, landscapes and miniatures; cabinets of china were inserted wherever possible and every sofa and chair had embroidered cushions. Beaded mats lay on the tables strewn with ornaments, and the reds and purples of the carpet struck the final note to the room of a wealth of ill-assorted colours.

At luncheon Louise sat one side of the General whilst Lucy, to her secret dismay, found herself between him and her hostess, on whose left sat Ludovic, with Katharine on his other side.

Mrs. Fyfield at once engaged Lucy in loud conversation. She was one of those people whose eyes perpetually wander when they are talking to anyone. Her eyes darted looks at the servants, then roved over Katharine and Ludovic, who seemed forced into making conversation to each other, neither having anything to say.

Turning to Lucy, she said, "I am sure you are good at embroidery and bead work, Miss Lucy."

Lucy looked startled. "I'm afraid I'm not," she said. "I never learnt. I can only do plain sewing for Missions or the poor whom Aunt Ada looks after."

"Then I shall ask you for some advice," said her hostess, "about the sort of stuff to get. Where does Ada get hers?"

"In Dashbury mostly."

Mrs. Wilson Fyfield opened her mouth to speak again, but what she was saying was lost in the loud tones of the conversation the General was having with Louise. He was very deaf and had presumably no idea of the volume of his voice.

"Sorry Hugh couldn't come today," he shouted. "I'd got a gun to show him. I suppose he's in London—doesn't seem to be here at all, always grubbing about in the City."

"Hugh is always very busy," said Louise vaguely.

"Not like a country gentleman at all," said the General, "yet he's a good man to hounds and a good shot. Well, I suppose he must do it to keep up a great barrack of a place like Dashbury. I don't know what the country's coming to."

Louise looked passive and unresponsive.

The General turned to Lucy. "D'you like dogs?" he asked.

"Yes, I do," she said.

The old spaniel looked up at her with bleary eyes. She put her hand on his head and he came closer to her.

"Taken a fancy to you, 'pon my word," said the General, and through the rest of the meal he continued a one-sided conversation with Lucy about his various dogs and horses.

His wife tried at moments to intervene, but he took no notice. She perforce had to turn and talk to Ludovic while Katharine made difficult conversation to Louise.

Ludovic's face did not betray his inward amusement and he held his hostess's attention by talking to her about the South of France.

Mrs. Wilson Fyfield leaned forward and tried to draw Katharine into her conversation with Ludovic. The luncheon was elaborate and long. Course succeeded course and Lucy, whose head had begun to ache from the heat of the room and the booming echo of the General's voice, wished herself back in her own little room at Dashbury.

Louise had turned her head towards her hostess and was listening to Ludovic talking. He seemed completely at his ease in contrast to Mrs. Fyfield's restless chatter and Katharine's uneasy attentiveness.

At long last Mrs. Fyfield rose to her feet after a glance at Louise, and led the ladies back into the drawing-room.

Louise seated herself on the sofa and glanced furtively at the clock on the mantelpiece. Lucy sat down and an embarrassing feeling of faintness crept over her. The room seemed to dissolve as she clutched the arms of the chair and shut her eyes.

Katharine came towards her and a smelling bottle was thrust under her nose. "I'm going to take Lucy up to my room," she said over her shoulder. "She's feeling faint." She pulled Lucy to her feet and, disregarding the exclamations of her elders, opened the door and with an arm round her shoulders drew Lucy into the hall. There was an aroma of damp fur from the many rugs on the marble floor, but its icy chill after the overheated drawing-room revived Lucy. Katharine firmly led her to the front door which she opened and they stood in the portico.

Lucy drew in a long breath of the cold afternoon freshness and the colour came back into her face.

"I'm better now," she said, as they stood together looking down a slope towards the valley.

"I thought you would be," said Katharine. "I can't stand that stuffy drawing-room myself. I often feel faint there too." She drew her arm through Lucy's. "Now come up to my room and lie down on my bed."

Katharine's room was far less full of objects than the room downstairs. It had a striped wallpaper and chintzes sprinkled with little bunches of roses. The walls were hung with small sporting prints and the windows looked out on the side of a hill crowned by a little beechwood which stood motionless in the sunshine.

"Now lie down on my bed, I'll take your shoes off."

"But I feel all right now."

"You'll feel better if you lie down for a few minutes."

Presently Mrs. Wilson Fyfield poked her head round the door. She ignored Lucy's recumbent figure on the bed.

"Katharine, your father wants you to take Ludovic to see the horses. Please put on your goloshes and your cape. I will look after Miss Lucy. How are you feeling, my dear?"

Lucy had risen from the bed. "Quite well, thank you," she said. "Please can I come down now?"

Katharine put on her goloshes and took her cape out of the cupboard. She looked cross and pulled at her cape with an angry jerk.

"Come down with me, Miss Lucy. Louise is talking to my husband. I should like to show you some flannel."

When Katharine came downstairs Ludovic was waiting for her in the hall. His face was a blankly polite mask. When, however, he had closed the hall door, for the first time that day he experienced a rise of spirits. After the stuffiness of the house reverberating with pointless talk, the afternoon, tranced in winter stillness, was refreshing and soothing. He glanced at Katharine, who did not appear to want to talk. 'I wonder how she can stand that stepmother of hers,' he thought.

Aloud he said, "Are you a great rider?"

"I am fond of riding," replied Katharine. "I've always done it, and it takes me out of the house into nice places. This is supposed to be good riding country."

They had reached the stables where two horses poked their heads over the top of the door of their stalls. Katharine pushed aside the head of one of them, who, scenting the lumps of sugar she had taken out of her pocket, tried to get in first for his share.

"Will you keep Firefly off?" she said. "He's pretty greedy, and I want to give Ranger his share."

89

Ludovic put his hand on to the satin-smooth neck of Firefly and held him off while Katharine fed Ranger. She looked at Ludovic and he at her and they both smiled as the horses, seeing that no more sugar was forthcoming, turned back to their stalls.

Ludovic would have lingered in the neat stable yard, but Katharine said, "I think we ought to go back. Lucy can't want to look at charity materials for long," and they both laughed in a pleasant complicity of things unsaid.

Meanwhile Lucy, revived by fresh air and her brief rest, was ushered down a stone back stairs, through stone-flagged passages smelling of paraffin as they passed a shelf on which stood a number of lamps with china globes, into a small dark room where bales of red flannel and cotton stuffs were stacked on a small table beside a sewing machine.

Mrs. Wilson Fyfield said, "This is where I keep my charity materials, but I am not satisfied with this last lot. Do please feel the stuff and tell me whether you think it is good or whether what they have in Dashbury is better."

Lucy drew the bale of flannel towards her and took a piece between her thumb and finger. She could find nothing the matter with it. "I think this stuff is good," she said gravely, "it should wear well. Does Katharine do your cutting out?"

"No, Katharine is no good at it at all. My maid does it."

They returned to the drawing-room. Louise had risen to her feet. "Are you quite recovered, Lucy?" she asked.

"Yes," said Lucy, "I only felt faint for a moment."

The General remarked kindly that he for his part often felt deuced queer in the drawing-room. "Theresa keeps this room like a greenhouse."

At that moment Katharine and Ludovic came in bringing a waft of outside freshness with them. Katharine's cheeks were a little flushed. She walked over to Lucy.

"Is the carriage there?" said Louise.

"It is just coming round," replied Ludovic.

Theresa Wilson Fyfield followed them to the door. The two elder ladies bade each other farewell with a flawless courtesy on Louise's side and strident effusiveness on her hostess's.

"Do come over again, Ludovic," said Theresa.

Ludovic thanked her and followed Louise and Lucy into the brougham.

The winter afternoon was still softly bright and a light mist rose from the river. The horses went off smartly as if glad to be going home, their hoofs ringing with a hollow sound as they passed over the bridge.

Louise drew her cape round her and closed her eyes. Ludovic, who was sitting with his back to the horses, made a face at Lucy and stared out of the window.

Louise, who had spoken no word during the drive, went straight up to her bedroom on her return.

Ludovic remarked that he was half asleep and that he should go out in the garden. "Come along," he said to Lucy, "and get some air."

As they went out it was beginning to freeze again.

"Hurry," said Ludovic, and they ran along the terrace through a door and back in at the front door and into the hall. Then Lucy disappeared upstairs.

19

LUDOVIC went into the drawing-room. Hugh was standing by the fireplace talking to a young man who was listening to him with an air of deferential attention.

Ludovic shook hands with him, and as he did so Ada came into the room.

"Ada, you haven't yet met Mr. Albert Grainger," said Hugh. "This is my sister, Miss Taynton."

Ada gave him a swift appraising glance and seated herself behind the tea urn, remarking that Louise had sent a message to say that she had a headache and was not coming down to tea.

"Come and sit next to me, Mr. Grainger," she said.

Albert Grainger complied. At that moment Lucy came in.

"I am so sorry to be late," she said, "but Aunt Louise wanted me."

"This is Miss Lucy Taynton," said Hugh.

Mr. Grainger's eyes rested for a moment upon Lucy, who came to stand beside Ada to hand round the teacups. Ada took a piece of bread and butter and seemed prepared for conversation. No one seeing Albert Grainger for the first time would have guessed his inward feelings.

His father had died young and his mother had brought him up in genteel poverty. His uncle, the retiring land agent at Dashbury, had taken an interest in the boy as he had grown up, and thought him sharp and intelligent with a good head for business and had recommended him to Hugh as his successor. He himself was going to live in the town of Dashbury and therefore could help the young man to grasp the estate business from nearby.

He had discussed the members of the Dashbury family

with his nephew. They would have been shocked and not a little surprised had they heard the latest conversation between the older and younger man over their port and walnuts in Mr. Grainger's small dining-room.

"It's a good job," he had said, "if you play your cards well. I've put up with snubs and slights, and you will have to do the same and look as if you didn't notice or didn't mind."

Young Albert Grainger looked sulky for a moment, then he said smoothly, "There's always some disadvantage in any job, Uncle. I expect I can put up with it if I must."

Mr. Grainger swallowed a mouthful of port. "His lordship's not an easy man, he can be peremptory and harsh, and he dislikes being contradicted. . . . But he's a just man, I will say that, and if you stand up to him over any matter he'll come round in time." Mr. Grainger paused. "And if you can make him think that something you want done is his own idea, that helps——"

The young man listened silently as he twisted the stem of his empty glass round and round.

"I can always tell you more about this when you begin your work . . . you can come and consult me at Dashbury, only don't say much about it. I don't want his lordship to think that you are always coming for advice to me behind his back."

"And the ladies of the family?" Albert asked.

The elder Mr. Grainger leant back in his chair. "Now you're asking," he said.

"Will they be nice to Mother?"

"Yes, and no. In their own high and mighty way, yes, and they'll send her grapes and game, but she'll get no further with them. . . . Mind you," he added, as he reached for a walnut from the bowl in the centre of the table, "now

93

old Lady Dashbury, she's an invalid, but she wants to go back to her house in the park as soon as she can—I always got on well with her. She's good and true, a word from me to her would often have good results with this man and his father. She'll help your mother—help her a lot if she lives. The present Lady D. is quite another pair of shoes. She isn't exactly insolent, but she can look straight through you till you feel as if you weren't there. Watch your step with her, she's not happy, I fancy, and she doesn't put herself about for other people. She never says quite what she means and will do things that you don't expect—and Miss Ada——" He stared in front of him.

"She looks rather a tartar," said Albert.

"A tartar she is, and no mistake. Folks who want to make up to her say that she lives for others." The tone in which this was said carried no hint of approval.

"And does she . . . I mean, live for others?"

"Well, she does a great deal for the poor round here in the two villages, but they don't care for her though they're civil enough to her face for what they can get from the big house. But when she brings them soup and blankets she stuffs a tract into their hands and asks them how they are getting on with their Bible readings, and why little Tommy wasn't at the last Sunday School. She is inclined to interfere and she's always trying to save the servants; most of them are underworked and overfed, if you ask me. But as long as you're polite and ask her opinion about things she'll be all right. The person who matters to you next to his lordship is Ludovic; he's no easy proposition and it's him you'll have to look out for in the long run. Ludovic is a dark horse to have come out of that stable. He and his uncle are like oil and water. He's interested in books and pictures and such like, gets bored with business pretty quickly, and I have a feeling, but mum's the word about this, that he won't want to live here when he succeeds to the title." Mr. Grainger cracked another walnut.

"I think Lord Dashbury feels this though he doesn't put it into words. When he dies you would have a good chance of getting a lot of things into your own hands here as Master Ludovic will probably go off to Italy for long spells. I don't know," he paused, "but this will all need great care as Ludovic isc lever and doesn't let you know what he's thinking. Sometimes he pounces on something when you think he hasn't been noticing anything at all."

Albert sat straight up in his chair. His face showed very little of what he was thinking. He was confident in his powers of handling people and thoughts raced through his head. "I shall not forget a word you have said, Uncle," he remarked after a minute or two, "and by the way, what about that girl Lucy Taynton?"

"Well, she's just a poor relation who does what she's told. I have hardly even spoken to her, but she looks a nice enough girl."

This and many other talks with his uncle had sunk deeply into Albert's mind. He was privately determined to go his own way at Dashbury Park, but he filed his uncle's remarks away in his mind for future reference.

As tea progressed he remembered that he was not going to be overawed, but that it was necessary to look overawed. He would have liked to stare round the room at the gods and goddesses disporting themselves on the ceiling and to take in the complicated array of china and silver on the table at which he sat. But he kept his eyes fixed on Ada, who was enquiring whether his mother was High or Low Church. (This was a question about which he had been forewarned by his uncle.) He replied, choosing his words carefully, that his mother would no doubt attend the church at Belling, though later she might like occasionally to visit

Dashbury Church. This answer seemed to satisfy Ada, and Albert was careful not to add that in the north of England town where his mother lived she often attended chapel services although she was nominally a member of the Church of England; she found their services heartier and the people more friendly than those in the neighbouring church. Albert did not wish his mother to come to Dashbury with the faintest taint of nonconformity attached to her.

He looked across the table to where Ludovic and Lucy were sitting. They had fallen silent and seemed occupied with their own thoughts. Ludovic wore a slight frown and Lucy's face a remote brooding look. Albert stared at them with the look of an actor who meets his fellow players in a company for the first time. He pulled himself up as Ada was asking him another question.

Bourton came in and approaching Ludovic said that his lordship wished to see him and Mr. Grainger in the study. Albert rose thankfully to his feet while Ludovic's face hardened into boredom.

Ada visited her sister-in-law after tea. Louise, wrapped in a *negligée* with falls of lace at the neck and sleeves, was sniffing a small bottle of smelling salts. She looked up languidly when Ada came in.

"How is your head?" Ada enquired.

"A little better," she replied. "The drawing-room at Widcote was so very hot and Dick and Theresa are such tiring people, even Lucy felt faint. Then Theresa took her away to look at some charity materials for her Guild, and I was left with Dick, who is deafer than ever, and his voice is so loud, too; while as for Theresa's voice, it just goes straight through your head."

"How did Ludovic get on?"

Louise closed her eyes in an effort to think. "Theresa

seemed to want him to talk to Katharine. She sent her out
to show him the stables."

Their eyes met. "Ah yes, I see," said Ada. "She wants
Ludovic for Katharine: she's always been such a match-
maker. It would suit her book very well to get her foot in
here.... Does Ludovic show any signs of liking Katharine?"

"You never can tell with Ludovic—he was very polite
and tried to talk to the girl while Theresa talked to Lucy,
until Dick found out that Lucy liked dogs and went on and
on about them, leaving me out. It was all very tiresome and
tiring, and it gave me this headache." Her eyelids fluttered
and the smelling bottle again came into play.

"What is Katharine like?" Ada persisted, ignoring these
symptoms of dismissal. "She seemed shy and awkward
when she came here."

Louise sat up on the sofa. "She would be good-looking
if she was better dressed."

"Did she seem to like Ludovic?"

"Really, Ada, I couldn't possibly tell: it was all so hot
and noisy and tiring. I really think I must rest now." She
rearranged the cushions behind her back. "I can never tell
what Ludovic is thinking about. I can't understand him at
all. He's not impertinent or off-hand, but I never get to
know him any better; sometimes I feel that he thinks what
I say is quite ridiculous or silly. He doesn't show it openly
—I just feel it."

"I can't understand him either," said Ada.

Louise closed her eyes as a broad hint that their conversation should come to an end. Ada waited for a moment,
then rose and abruptly opened the door, closing it behind
her with a noise which drew an exclamation of annoyance
from her sister-in-law.

20

L<small>UCY</small> had brought the book of Stevenson's essays to
Jane Dashbury, who examined it with interest.

"Let's start reading it," she said. "Have you looked at it?"

"Yes, I have read the first two essays."

In silence Lucy tendered George's letter to her.

"A charming letter, my dear. We'll read one of the essays
this evening, then you can write and tell Mr. Maxwell how
much we are enjoying the book."

Lucy sat silent and embarrassed.

Jane Dashbury remarked, "Ludovic brought the book
and letter to you here. I take it he didn't mention it to anyone else."

"No, I don't think he did."

"Well, we'll leave it at that. If anyone sees us reading it
I shall say that Mr. Maxwell sent this book and that I am
greatly enjoying it."

Jane Dashbury sighed a little. She thought, 'I would
give much for Lucy to be happy—as long as I am here I
shall see that no one stops this budding friendship, if I can
prevent it. From what Ludovic tells me I am sure that they
would suit each other, and I should not die feeling that Lucy
would get older in this house doing odd jobs for other
people and with no prospect of a home of her own.' These
thoughts came and went in a flash.

Lucy looked up and saw Jane smiling at her. "Run along
now and when you write your letter bring it back to me: it
shall go with one or two of mine. I always enclose them in a
large envelope and Soey slips them into the postbag. Tell
Mr. Maxwell that Hugh hopes he will come back again and
look at the library."

Nothing more was said by either the old or young woman, and Lucy's short letter was duly written and sent.

When Ludovic came into the dining-room a few days later to breakfast he was smiling but gave no explanation of his unusual cheerfulness.

"Can I speak to you, Uncle Hugh?" he said.

When he entered the library he looked subdued but happy. "I had a letter from my chief this morning; one of the Embassy secretaries is ill, and he would like me to cut short my time here and go back to Rome as soon as I can."

Hugh frowned and then sighed. "You must go," he said, "if Sir Donald wants you. I can't pretend that it is convenient at this moment, just as young Grainger is taking over from his uncle; neither he nor you have begun to grasp the business of our East End London property or the leases of the houses in Dashbury or the problems here. On the other hand if you could come back in two months' time Grainger's nephew will know the work and we can get along quicker and I think that you would probably find it all easier to grasp. We don't seem to get on very quickly at the moment."

"I really have tried to give my mind to the business, Uncle Hugh."

"Yes, I believe you have, but your heart's not in it. When do you wish to go?"

"As soon as may be."

"Well, I'll talk to Grainger today and tell him to have the work in shape to show you when you get back. Have you said anything to your aunt about leaving?"

"No, I've said nothing about it to anyone."

"Well, go and tell her now."

The door closed. Hugh walked to the window and stared over the garden at the contours of the stretch of grass bordered by trees. After a few moments he came back to his

99

writing table, sat heavily down and put his head in his hands. Then he rose and gave the hanging bell-pull by the mantelpiece a sharp tug.

Ludovic, when the door closed, cut a caper which had more gaiety than dignity about it. He then walked across the hall and through the drawing-room into his aunt's sitting-room. Louise had just finished interviewing Mrs. Robson, who departed by another door, slate in hand, the menus for the day inscribed on it.

Ludovic briefly said his say and Louise listened, her head inclined while she drew a profile on the blotting paper in front of her. "I'm sorry you are going," she said without lifting her head. "I'm afraid it's been dull for you here with all that business to do and no balls or dinner parties. In the spring we must try and get some people of your own age to come. Hugh seems uncertain as to whether we can go to London in the summer, but I do hope we can."

Ludovic had just caught sight of Lucy through the french window, hurrying along to give a message to Mundell the head gardener, who had paused while crossing the terrace garden.

"Thank you very much, Aunt Louise," said Ludovic. "I shall look forward to seeing you in the spring. I've just seen Lucy in the garden so I think I will run out and tell her and then go up and see Grandmamma."

Louise sighed a little as she watched him run hatless down the steps and clear the flower beds with a series of flying leaps. Her mind was not given to metaphor, but if it had been she might have thought that youth took life in a series of leaps while middle age kept to the sure centre of a flat road.

When Ludovic reached Lucy, Mundell touched his cloth cap. He regarded Ludovic with interest and with that slightly suspicious malevolence that gardeners, whose whole life is spent in fighting the weather, are apt to show. Mundell's soul was seared by the recollection of a hailstorm the previous May which had ravaged the fruit blossom and the unexpectedly early frost which had blackened the dahlias, and the predatory and ungrateful birds who were pampered with crumbs by Miss Ada and Miss Lucy, and then had fallen upon the early peas, or the slugs and snails who had advanced in their legions seeking what they might devour. His life moved slowly in a sort of commination service. He liked few human beings, but Lucy had gained some slight favour in his eyes by her gentle sympathy with his griefs, and he sometimes gave her a bunch of flowers saying, "For yourself, Miss."

As much as possible he made the Dashburys feel that while they might own the garden and pay for its upkeep, he was commander-in-chief of the forces, and that even the smallest plum and the most minute clump of pansies or the most casually blooming rose should be disposed of according to his wishes. His under-gardeners and gardeners' boys worked harder than any others in the neighbourhood, feeling like small animals with a hawk hovering over them ready to pounce.

At this precise moment Lucy had been conveying a message from Louise, who wanted more begonias and geraniums, as she was displeased by the colour of the cinerarias. Mundell recognised the necessity of bringing indoors plants for the decoration of the house; but when would her ladyship realise that greenhouses are not florists' shops, and that some plants lag behind others in their growth and do not always bloom true to type?

Lucy had finished delivering her message and thanked Mundell, who walked away with the flat-footed gait peculiar to gardeners. The two young people turned back towards the house.

"I'm going back to Rome."

Lucy stopped and stared at him. "How pleased you look. I am glad for you, but I shall miss you."

Ludovic looked startled, he had not thought of this or of any feelings but his own.

"When are you going?"

"In a few days, but I shall come back in the spring."

To Lucy the spring seemed a long way off as she glanced at the landscape iron-bound by winter all around her.

"You must go and see Cousin Jane and tell her," she said.

Ludovic's exuberant gaiety had evaporated by the time he reached Jane Dashbury's room and he walked in soberly to see her. When he had told her she said, "My dear boy, I am glad in a way though I am going to miss you; it's been so nice having you coming up to see me." He fell silent for a moment. "Well the spring will be here soon and you will return when the flowers are out and everything looks more cheerful. I should like to see you as often as I can before you leave."

When Soey was told of Ludovic's impending departure she remarked with a particular kind of sniff, which she well knew how to use to denote disapproval: "Fidgety, that's what he is, always on the go . . . stands to reason that he won't settle down here . . . him being a bit of a foreigner . . . his mother was a sweet lady when she came, but couldn't seem to take to anything and her French maid—a more poor ignorant creature I've never set eyes on—didn't seem to understand anything and couldn't seem to like to eat the food here—said it didn't taste of anything. . . . Well, we all have our little ways but there's no doubt ours are best. . . ."

Ludovic found to his surprise that he was invaded by a sense of discomfort which increased steadily each day. It focused itself upon Lucy and his grandmother. He knew that his visits had been an interlude to them both, a stave of lighter music in a heavy symphony.

Hugh refrained from any more comments. He merely said that he hoped young Grainger would be more conversant with the work by the time Ludovic returned.

21

LUDOVIC sat in his bedroom. He had flung his dressing-gown on but seemed in no hurry to go to bed. He sat frowning and recalling that he had arrived from Italy with the firm determination to make it clear to his uncle that he had no intention of ever taking over Dashbury and its responsibilities.

The weeks had slipped past, each with its own weight of difficulty—he was no nearer telling Hugh what he had meant to tell him. An unwilling respect and liking for his uncle had crept into his mind as day followed day.

He rose and paced up and down the room. He pulled open the heavy curtains and stood gazing down at the park, moonlit and silent, and at the pattern of pointed shadows which lay on the grass from the four cypress trees planted at the angles round the fountain.

The profound stillness outside was accentuated in the phantom sound of a mouse behind the skirting board or the droning of a belated fly round the lamp. The scene was set for clear and decisive meditation, but Ludovic closed the curtains, seated himself in an armchair by the dying fire, then, abruptly extinguishing both lamp and bedside candle, flung himself into his bed.

He slept fitfully, teased by a kaleidoscope of dreams which dissolved before they had worked themselves out. He seemed to be sitting in the dining-room at the head of the table. Someone had handed him a plate full of soup—there were other people he did not recognise sitting at the table, and a figure at the other end whom he was on the point of recognising when the dream was succeeded by another one and he found himself on a shore where a blue sea murmured and small waves ran up on the yellow sands. He was conscious of a lightness of heart and a sense of happy expectancy, someone who made for his happiness was coming to meet him there; then he was walking in a wood shot with sunlight and as he went on the trees crowded together, the sunlight waned and the way became more difficult. He stumbled over a rock and woke up crying out that he was lost.

The room was silent and dark and he turned over and fell into a dreamless sleep.

After breakfast he asked, "Do you want me in the library, Uncle Hugh?"

Hugh looked at Ludovic over the top of his newspaper. "No, I don't think so," he replied, "there is nothing special for you to do this morning."

Louise left the dining-room followed by Ada and the two young people.

Ada said over her shoulder, "Lucy, I shall want you at ten-thirty." She managed to convey an atmosphere of disapproval.

"Come and talk to me till then, Lucy," said her cousin. "We shan't have many more chances." They went into the drawing-room and stood by the fire.

"I'll write to you," said Ludovic, "and send you some

books, and you'll write to me too, won't you? I want to hear about Grandmamma and her health."

There was a pause. Ludovic looked at Lucy.

"George sent you a Louis Stevenson book, didn't he? We read one or two of them when I was at Oxford. I think he made a good choice in sending you a book which takes you into a different world, to the coast of Scotland, quite unlike the stuffy gorgeousness of this house, and more bracing."

He looked round the long room and down to the flowered, rose-tinted carpet at his feet. The morning light coming in through the long windows shone impartially on all the tables, inlaid cabinets and large and small chairs. Lucy stood still and silent by the fire.

"I shall have two days in London," continued Ludovic, "and I may be able to run down to Oxford for the day and lunch in college with George. Have you any message for him?"

Lucy coloured but still said nothing.

"Well," he said with slight impatience, "I can say, can't I, that you have enjoyed the book?"

"Yes, please do, and Cousin Jane has enjoyed it too."

"Well I shall tell him that, and that you will help him in the library when he comes back here."

Lucy nodded, still consumed by her shyness.

"By the way," he said, "I've got one or two books with me here that you can read and keep for me. I'll put them in your room."

Lucy vigorously shook her head. "No, please don't. Aunt Ada might come in and see them."

"But she won't bother about them: she never reads anything herself except the Bible and tracts."

"No, but that's why she thinks other books are unsuitable. She just looks at their covers and then makes guesses."

"Poor Lucy," said Ludovic. "Well, I know what I'll do. I'll take them along to Grandmamma's room: it's a sort of sanctuary in this house."

Ludovic came into his grandmother's room carrying an armful of books.

"Can I leave them here?" he said. "I think I can fit them into your bookcase. I thought you might like to look at them, and Lucy too."

He smiled down at her and a flicker of understanding passed between them. No more was said as he pushed them into the shelves.

Ada remarked at luncheon: "I hear that you are going away, Ludovic. You will enjoy the gaieties of Rome after the quiet life here."

'Just what does she mean by that?' thought Ludovic. 'Does she think that life here is quiet, with all of us watching each other all the time? It's "Can I say this, that or the other to Aunt Louise? Oh, Aunt Ada will be shocked if I say that—watch your words with Uncle Hugh in case he thinks you frivolous or stupid." Lucy and Grandmamma are the only people to whom I can talk freely.'

22

THE winter was a long one. The forces of spring retreated against nipping frost, mist and cold. In spite of this discouragement the late afternoons showed a slight but continuous lightening, and a breath of something better to come. The evening dusk no longer came so early and spearheads of spring in little groups of bulbs came sturdily up through the dark earth. Snowdrops and aconites stood in drifts below the bare twigs of the shrubberies at the edge of the terraced garden.

One morning Louise received a letter from Mrs. Wilson Fyfield which contained a lengthy explanation about her and her husband being invited to take their horses and to go and stay for a week's hunting in another part of the county. Katharine was not invited; might she possibly, if it was convenient, come and stay at Dashbury?

'I wonder if Theresa thinks that Ludovic is here?' thought Louise.

Jane Dashbury received the news with approval. "It will be nice for Lucy to have someone of her own age."

"Oh, yes," said Louise, "I suppose it will," and then, seeing the slight lift of her mother-in-law's delicate eyebrows, she repeated: "Yes, of course it will be nice for Lucy. I will put Katharine into the room next to hers."

"Yes, do so, my dear, girls love to chatter till all hours."

Louise looked surprised. It had never occurred to her that Lucy had anything to chatter about.

The Wilson Fyfields departed for their visit, and Katharine came to stay at Dashbury. She arrived at tea-time and she and Lucy were then allowed to go up to her bedroom.

Katharine's clothes were being unpacked and Lucy drew her into her own bedroom next door.

"This is nice," Katharine said, "it's fun to be with someone young."

Lucy, who was trying to encourage the fire in the small grate to burn, looked up. "Yes," she said, "until Ludovic came, I'd never known a person younger than myself."

Katharine moved to the dressing-table and examined a small tortoiseshell brush with a monogram on it.

"Do you like him? Ludovic, I mean?"

107

"Oh, yes, indeed I do," said Lucy. "He's been so kind to me and has made me laugh such a lot. . . . I wish," she added with a sigh as she wrestled with a lump of coal which refused either to burn or to be broken up by the poker, but sat sullenly amidst the glowing embers, "Yes, I wish that he was happier here. He doesn't care for Dashbury, but he's only seen it in the winter and it's been so cold, and he's had so much business to do. He's worked such a lot with Uncle Hugh."

"Doesn't he like work?" said Katharine. She had taken up the brush and was examining it.

"He likes some sort of work. The Ambassador at Rome told Uncle Hugh that he works much harder than honorary attachés usually do, and he's very interested in the antiquities of Rome."

At that moment Ada marched in without knocking. She looked at Katharine.

Lucy spoke. "Katharine's unpacking is being done," she said.

"I hope you haven't brought a large wardrobe," said Ada, "we live very quietly here."

"I haven't got many dresses, Miss Taynton," said Katharine. Ada had brought an awkwardness into the room with her and Katharine looked petrified by shyness.

"Well, don't be late for dinner," said Ada over her shoulder as she left the room, shutting the door smartly behind her.

Katharine and Lucy looked at each other.

"Is she always like that?" whispered Katharine.

"She is rather . . . well, like that," replied Lucy in the same low tone.

Katharine was taken to Belling Church on Sunday. Ada marched up the aisle in front of the two girls and they followed her into the first pew below the pulpit.

The service was conducted rapidly and with a sad lack of feeling for the rhythm and beauty of what was read. But there was sincerity in the heart of the clergyman, and the sermon he preached would have reached his congregation's minds and hearts if he had had more skill in developing his theme. As it was he lost his way, and concluded in a welter of meaningless sentences.

Katharine looked at Lucy, who sat quite still gazing upwards at the preacher with a serious look on her face. Lucy had been trained by her father to listen to sermons and to remember the text on which the discourse was based, and also to discuss the content with him afterwards. She showed more interest than the rest of the congregation who mostly abstracted their minds, pursued as they were even in church by the strains and troubles of everyday life. Katharine tried to listen, but her mind persisted in wandering back to her first visit to Dashbury and to Ludovic's carelessly flung-out questions. And then their walk together to the stables at Widcote when Ludovic, thankful to have escaped the oppressive politeness of her stepmother, had become gentler and less formidable, and for a short time they had talked cheerfully together.

At the end of the service the congregation went out, scraping their feet on the cold stone floor of the church. They held back and stood silent while Ada had a word to say to the clergyman's wife.

"She behaves like the queen," thought Katharine, as Ada progressed along the mossy path which led to the lychgate.

Mr. Grainger and his nephew were standing by the gate. The older man removed his hat, which he had crammed down on to his head as his hair was thinning and the wind was cold.

He greeted Ada with great *empressement* and enquired if he and his nephew might walk a little way with them.

Albert was introduced to Katharine and he took his place between the two girls. He looked at Katharine and said,

"You come from this part of the world, Miss Wilson Fyfield?"

"Yes I do, from Widcote, about five miles away."

They walked along and Lucy tried to think of something which would mutually interest her companions.

"Have you got a horse yet?" she asked, quickening her pace a little.

"My uncle lends me his. It's stout and rather old, but I'm thankful for that as I don't know how I should manage a more mettlesome steed."

Katharine, who had ridden first ponies and then horses ever since she could remember anything at all about her childhood, opened her eyes in amusement.

There was a slight jauntiness about Albert Grainger which did not match Katharine's tongue-tied silence. Lucy had, early in her life, been schooled in making conversation to her fellow villagers and had had the task of welding small sewing meetings and village tea parties into some kind of unity. This had been no easy task in a community where each individual had an encyclopaedic knowledge of each other's circumstances, moral and financial, and where a chance remark would be remembered and commented upon long after the occasion on which it was uttered had passed.

So as they walked along Lucy exerted herself to find some common conversational ground between her two companions. To her relief Ada and the elder Grainger parted when the house came in sight. Ada walked on quickly.

"Do you like that man, Lucy?" asked Katharine. "You seemed to have plenty to say to him."

"Well, as you were completely silent," replied Lucy, "I felt I had to talk, you can't just walk along and say nothing."

Katharine stopped and stared at Lucy. "You're just like my stepmother," she said, "she's always saying that I must talk."

Lucy laughed. The idea that she in any way resembled Mrs. Wilson Fyfield was comical in the extreme, and Katharine, after looking at her for a moment, laughed too.

Ada turned her head and beckoned to them to walk faster and the girls followed her with sobered faces. It would be impossible to explain their mirth to Ada.

That evening before dinner Katharine asked Lucy to lend her one or two books. "I'm so ignorant," she said. "I never learnt anything really in the schoolroom, but no governess lasted long: my stepmother couldn't get on with them and just as I was beginning to learn something they left. I never got beyond the Saxon Kings in history; we were always going back to the beginning. . . ."

"Oh, poor Katharine, did you like any of your governesses?"

"Yes, I liked Mademoiselle, and I got a bit further with her, but my stepmother and she had endless rows and she left. She still writes to me sometimes."

"Why don't you go on with some French grammar? I mean, make a start that way, and then go on to other things?"

"You mean go on as if I was still in the schoolroom?"

"But the schoolroom is the start of things, surely," said Lucy.

"My stepmother would say that this was nonsense. She thinks you must pick up a smattering of things there and that that's all that matters. She doesn't mind if you never get properly taught anything, because she says that men like girls who aren't clever."

"But doesn't your father want you to learn things?"

"Oh no, he doesn't care, as long as I have a good seat on

a horse and ride well to hounds; he thinks that that's more important than anything except shooting and dogs . . .."

Lucy looked enquiring and surprised.

"Do you think my stepmother is right?"

Lucy sat, chin in hand. Of the men she knew, her father, Ludovic, and George Maxwell, all had expected her to read and be interested in the things of the mind. Uncle Hugh, well Uncle Hugh didn't ever read anything but the newspapers and dull-looking documents; she couldn't imagine his minding whether you did or didn't read books. True he knew she was bookish, and he had sent for her to the library to help George Maxwell. She sat lost in thought.

"You look very serious," said Katharine.

"I'm thinking it over," she said as she took up the needle-work that was lying in her lap. "My father encouraged me to read," she said, "and we used to read together." She paused and gave a sigh, "Then Ludovic lent me books and we talked about them, then . . ."

"Yes?"

"Well, his friend, Mr. Maxwell, who is an Oxford don, when he was here, let me help in the library, and Ludovic and he and I had a talk one evening after tea mostly about Sir Walter Scott—it was lovely—I mean it was nice."

"But weren't you afraid of talking to a clever old gentle-man?"

"Mr. Maxwell isn't old," said Lucy, "he's thirty, I think."

"Oh, I see," said Katharine.

23

SOEY looked crosser than ever. Jane Dashbury, Lucy thought, a little frailer and more transparent. "She's like a glass globe with a candle flame burning in it," she said to herself.

"How are you, Cousin Jane?" she asked timidly.

"Rather full of aches and pains, dear, but the doctor says that there's nothing to be done about it, so don't let's talk about it. I shall be better in the spring when I get to the Dower House."

Soey came in at that moment. "The workmen say that they'll be out in a month's time, m'lady."

Soey, whose acquaintance with the workmen had been a long one, refused to call them by their family or Christian names.

"That will be very nice," said Jane. "Spring is coming and I look forward to my flowers."

Soey gave her a look of mixed indulgence and exasperation and left the room.

The winter still beat back the forces of spring, and life at Dashbury Park went on like a wheel turning on its own axis day after day.

Mealtimes succeeded each other, daily duties were punctually fulfilled. Lucy was busy with Ada, who was planning as her principal activity in the early summer a meeting in London which necessitated a great deal of writing and checking through pamphlets to be sent out.

Ada had announced that she had been made Vice-Chairman. "This means a lot more work, Lucy. I hope you are prepared to do it well."

Lucy had received a letter from Ludovic that morning

from Rome, and her mind was elsewhere. "I'll do my best, Aunt Ada," she said.

Ada had a vague feeling of disappointment. She had hoped to impress the girl with her new importance, but Lucy, though polite, was neither eager nor responsive.

Ludovic's letter was graphic and interesting. He described places and people well and vividly.

"It isn't always warm here," he wrote, "but it never seems to be dark and dull and grey like it is with you at Dashbury. Things here happen oddly and amusingly, not at set times, though of course in the Embassy things move in routine. The odd thing is that I find myself wondering if everything is really going on just the same at Dashbury. Does Bourton ring the dressing gong at precisely the same time, and do Aunt Louise and Aunt Ada play cribbage when Uncle Hugh isn't there? Or have I imagined the whole thing? Perhaps it is like something in the Arabian Nights—I mean like the things Aladdin conjured up which all looked so real and yet which vanished in a puff.

"But all this is nonsense. The real news that I have is that I went to Oxford for a day and saw George. He is very busy with a book he is writing, as well as his pupils. But we lunched in his rooms and he talked about Dashbury. He is much too Scotch and reserved to say much but he seems to have enjoyed himself, and I think that he can do a lot more in the library, although he says it should be properly put straight by someone who could work much harder at it than he can. He said he would think of somebody to advise about this if Uncle Hugh wishes it. 'Miss Lucy could help,' he said. 'How is she? Is she well?' I said you were well, and as usual spending your time doing things for everyone else. 'She's too good for that sort of thing and because she's so good she does it so uncomplainingly.' Time flies here in Rome. One goes from one thing to another, but at

Dashbury old gentleman Time moves slowly along. He must be bored with his task."

Lucy put her letter away to read and read again. Letters were to her anyhow a very surprising form of communication and this one was like someone talking directly to the reader.

The days lengthened, trees lost their angularity, and their outlines became softer and fuzzier as the buds appeared.

Mundell grudgingly produced some pots of coloured hyacinths for the house and Lucy found some primroses with very short stalks under a bank. Their subtle and elusive scent gave them a value that the carpets of scentless snowdrops and aconites, lovely and welcome as they were, could not emulate. Jane was lying with her eyes closed when Lucy came in, but she roused herself to bury her face in the soft fragrance from outdoors.

Soey went about her work of looking after her mistress lightened neither in countenance nor clothes. She always held by the old saw 'Ne'er cast a clout till May is out', even on an April day of unseasonable mildness. The draughts in rooms diminished a little; Ada began to complain of stuffiness and flung windows open to let the sharp air in on the back of Louise's neck, who shivered gracefully and left the room.

George Maxwell wrote asking to come if Hugh would like him to do some work at Dashbury.

"It will be dull for him here without Ludovic," said Louise.

"Well, he knows what it's like here. If he wants to come it is because he's interested in the books," said Hugh curtly.

Lucy listened to this conversation with feelings of alarm. She could not and did not explain to herself that when your thoughts are dwelling upon another person and you are weaving a cocoon of fantasy about them, the return of this person into your life may well tear this cocoon into shreds, and leave nothing but a daunting reality in its place.

Without Ludovic there was no one with any thought or sympathy for her. What would happen? Probably nothing, and the year would go on again and the dull daily routine resume its sway.

The date of George Maxwell's visit was fixed by Hugh. He told Lucy briefly about it and said that she would help in the library when George needed it.

Ada frowned. "I shall want Lucy too," she said. "This will be a very busy time with me."

Hugh regarded his sister over the top of his newspaper. "Lucy must be there if Mr. Maxwell wants lists made of the books. He's a very busy man and can only come for a few days at a time. Important as your work no doubt is, my dear Ada, you must do without Lucy's help for those days."

The words were delivered in unaccented tone. It was impossible to say whether Hugh was using his well-known weapon of sarcasm or not.

Lucy felt like a shuttlecock batted between two determined opponents.

On Monday after breakfast Louise had sat silent and abstracted, frowning down at a letter beside her on the table, written in a scrawling handwriting which overflowed from the horizontal in the middle of the page to the vertical down the sides of the paper. She came into the library where Hugh was reading a lengthy document. He looked up with a slight frown.

"Did you want to see me, my dear?" he asked.

Louise sank into an armchair by the fire and waited, tendering her letter as she did so.

"What's this?" he said. "Oh, Violet. What does she want?"

"You'll soon see," said Louise calmly. "She wants to come here to stay."

Hugh fumbled for his glasses and looked at the letter.

"Dashed if I can read it," he said. "Why can't she write legibly or not at all?"

"Shall I read it to you?"

"No, I'll read it to myself, thank you. Do you want her here?"

"Well, she is my own niece," said Louise. "She hasn't been here for over a year."

"Very well, my dear. Certainly invite her. Mr. Maxwell will be here then, but that doesn't matter. I don't think he and she would have much in common."

"Violet can always get on with any man," was Louise's unspoken comment. "Whatever they're like, they go down like ninepins in front of her."

Violet's arrival caused a stir of interest throughout the whole household, the same stir that the approach of a glittering fish might occasion to the torpid inhabitants of a tank, revolving with barely moving fins amongst softly heaving pond weed. Fresh curtains were put up in the room she would occupy, the frilled pincushion stood out starched and stiff, an intricate pattern of pins on its top and sides.

Mundell was made to bring in a pot of pink hyacinths, stiff as sentinels and surrounded by moss. They would of course have to be moved at night, it being well known that scented flowers threw out gases injurious to health in the hours of darkness. Mundell also brought in a nondescript plant of striped leaves which had to be put in a remote corner of the room.

Louise surveyed the room with satisfaction. Why did Violet want to come, she wondered, as she absently smoothed the grooved pillar in the fourposter bed with her fingers and thumb.

Violet must know that there was so little to entertain her at Dashbury. Louise had written to remind her that except for a neighbour or two there would be no company much of a lively sort, and Violet had replied in a letter nearly all dots and dashes that it would be heavenly to see her Uncle and Aunt and have a few days at lovely Dashbury before the London season began. London at that moment was both empty and dull.

Violet's relations and some of her friends read her letters between the lines as it were. They had discovered that the discrepancy between what she meant them to think and what she wrote was somewhat wide.

The evening before she came Bourton handed Louise a telegram, which looked small and insignificant on the large salver. Louise took it and read it through carefully twice.

"It's from Ludovic," she said. "He would like to come tomorrow, at the same time as Violet. He wants to stay for a fortnight. I must answer it. Get me a telegraph form, Bourton, please."

There was a silence in the room while she filled up the form and Bourton went off bearing it on the salver.

"Ludovic will be a help," she said, "while Mr. Maxwell is here, and he will entertain Violet." Then a thought seemed to strike her and she sat silent for a few minutes.

Lucy was thinking how nice it would be to see Ludovic and to have some more talks with him and George Maxwell. Ada had given an exclamation of surprise and possibly displeasure, but neither of the other two heeded her.

"Lucy, will you find Sarah and tell her to come and see me in the boudoir? Please tell her about Ludovic's room. I will put him next to Mr. Maxwell in the Green room."

The expected guests were arriving by the afternoon train coinciding with tea-time. Louise changed her dress and in the lamplight her pearls shone in a soft cluster at her throat.

Ada changed into an austere blue gown of no special shape, while Lucy put on a white collar to lighten her shabby black garment.

Tea minus the teapot and urn was brought in. Louise fidgeted a little, patting her perfectly arranged hair. Ada studied a pamphlet with an expression on her face of hardship nobly endured; and Lucy took up a piece of red flannel and put a few stitches into a petticoat.

A vague noise of opening doors was heard, a light laugh and some talk, and then Bourton flung the doors open and announced Lady Ashendon, Mr. Maxwell and Mr. Ludovic.

"What a delightful surprise meeting Ludovic in London. Darling Aunt Louise!" and Louise and her niece embraced.

"How are you, Violet?" she cried. "Well, I do hope."

"And dearest Uncle Hugh, how is he? He is so important that I never see him nowadays. Henry says he is so seldom at the Club; and Aunt Ada . . ." She turned towards Ada, who resisted her embrace, leaning her head rigidly backwards.

"And this is Lucy. I've heard about you. It is such a joy to be here after so long."

George Maxwell meanwhile shook hands with his hostess and looked a little stunned by the flood of exclamations.

He greeted Lucy when the party was about to be seated at the tea table. Their eyes met and to a very chance observer they would have seemed to meet for the first time as strangers.

Ludovic's greeting to Lucy was affectionate and warm but he slipped into the chair beside Violet and in a moment was engaged in talking to her. George, sitting between Louise and Ada, conversed with difficulty with both of them. They seemed to have very little to say to each other. Lucy had to replenish empty cups and pass plates, and cut cakes and generally to help.

When at last she sat down she took a long look at Violet. Violet was dressed in the height of fashion and her beauty seemed to match and be enhanced by the rich setting of the room. She turned the gaze of her lovely long-lashed eyes on Ludovic, smiled at Louise, darted a glance at George, and even gave Ada a look of embracing warmth.

Ada stared back, unable to retain her stony pose in face of all this warmth and gaiety. George looked at Violet and Lucy was conscious of a sharp pang of unhappiness, a feeling of apprehension, and of a menace to something of which she had thought and cherished as a dream.

Ludovic was exchanging joke for joke and Louise's colour had risen as she gestured a little with her long finely shaped hands.

When tea was cleared away Louise went off with Violet to her room. "How is Henry?" Louise asked.

"Darling Henry is very well. He sent you, oh! so many messages, dearest Aunt Louise."

When they reached the bedroom it showed mellow and glowing in the afternoon light. Violet was enchanted. She praised everything and remarked on the beauty of the hyacinths. Even the little odd-coloured plant came in for a word.

"We never have lovely ones like this at home," she said. Lord Ashendon, who took a personal interest in his greenhouses and was a carnation grower of some reputation, would not have been pleased to hear this.

Violet had married, very young, a man much older than herself. She had been the acknowledged beauty of a London season, had been talked about for constantly dancing with a good-looking but penniless Guardsman. And then, before the talk had died down, the announcement came in the *Morning Post* that Miss Violet Carey was engaged to the Earl of Ashendon. Gossip again passed round in the wide circle of hostesses and guests. Violet was censured for heartlessness by some. She had jilted a poor man for a rich one. What would she do next? The Guardsman transferred to a regiment in India, and Violet had a son after her first year of marriage and reappeared as the beautiful wife accompanied by a proud and devoted husband.

"We shall see what we shall see," the gossips said. Violet's parents, Sir Francis and Lady Carey, seemed delighted with their grandson, who remained with them for long periods of time. They made no comments on their daughter. They were not wealthy people and lived quietly in the country, only coming up to London for Sir Francis' visits to Tattersall's and to go to his Club, and for Lady Carey to do some shopping and theatres.

Violet was always warm in her welcome to dearest Papa and Mama and she was assiduous in asking her parents' friends to meals, while Henry Ashendon treated his father-and mother-in-law with kindness and courtesy. Returning home in the train Lady Carey wondered why she had not enjoyed her stay in London more. She tried to divert her mind from little Henry's visits to his mother's drawing-room and to forget the bewildered little face under the stream of unaccustomed endearments from a mother whom he saw only briefly and for whom he felt more disquiet than love.

She tried to avert her mind also from the thought of her nearest neighbours, whose daughters, plain and unfashionable, had married poor gentlemen with encumbered acres but in whose houses there existed a warm, unspoken love and trust between parents and children. Once when returning from London by a slow train that stopped at their little wayside station, tears came into Lady Carey's eyes. They brimmed over and ran down her cheeks. Her husband, who was dozing in the opposite corner of the railway carriage, opened his eyes suddenly and stared at her. Knowing how much he felt the Englishman's distaste for any display of emotion, she was about to grope in her reticule for a handkerchief when to her surprise he leant across the space between them and grasping her cold hands said:

"Yes, I know, my dear." He then leant back again in his seat, closing his eyes tightly and assuming a motionless pose.

His wife gazed out on the fields and hedges at the gathering darkness. She felt comforted and yet saddened. 'Francis knows,' she thought. 'I wonder where we went wrong in her upbringing.'

On her first evening at Dashbury Park Violet came down into the drawing-room a few minutes late. Her beauty had a kind of vividness. It did not only reside in the usual claim to that attribute. The curling brown hair, white brow and mouth like a cupid's bow, the brilliant young pink of her cheeks enhancing her dark eyes, her white shoulders and small waist would have delighted beholders. But there was also a feeling of vitality and of great pleasure in being alive that made Violet Ashendon the centre of any gathering like the heart of a cyclone. The envious and the admiring and the spiteful and censorious in what constituted London society could not deny this. She advanced into the room clasping her fan in her gloved hand, her skirts rustling, a confident smile on her face.

Ludovic's eyes were fixed on her, George gazed at her surprised, and the other ladies seemed to recede into the background.

Bourton's voice rang out behind Violet saying "Dinner is ready, your ladyship." This broke the spell, and Violet moved into dinner on Ludovic's arm.

After dinner, during which Lucy, seated between Ludovic and Ada, spoke very little, and Ada was in a monosyllabic mood, Ludovic turned a flushed and excited glance at Violet asking her questions and not heeding the answers. George conversed with Louise for a short time and then they all listened silently to Ludovic and Violet, whose flow of light talk ebbed to and fro.

After dinner Louise proposed a round game of cards. Lucy joined in the laughter and even Ada unbent slightly.

When the time came to go to bed and the ladies were taking the silver candlesticks in the hall preparatory to going upstairs, George came to where Lucy was standing, her candle illuminating her face, a little flush on her cheeks, her hair a little less neat than usual.

"May I hope for your help in the library tomorrow, Miss Lucy?" he said.

"Oh, yes," she said. Her face lit up with pleasure, as the candle flame flickered, casting light and shadow on his black-clad figure. Her hand suddenly was unsteady.

"I shall have to ask Aunt Ada, but I'm sure I can come."

Violet darted a glance at Lucy. The thought passed through her mind that Lucy was not quite so negligible as she had thought. Like all triumphant beauties she was quick to recognise the slightest shadow of competition with herself.

When Violet had said goodnight to Louise, and her maid had finished brushing her hair and removed her evening dress, she walked up and down the room, smiling to herself and humming a snatch of song with satisfaction. How clever she had been to find out quite by chance at a casual meeting with Ludovic that he would be visiting Dashbury at about this time. The visit to Dashbury was demanded of her as a family duty each year. She usually came there with her husband. This year Henry had to visit the north of England on business at this precise moment, and she had represented to him the idea that she could come without him and that she should fulfil her family duty alone. He acquiesced in this and she came, looking forward to pursuing a further acquaintance with Ludovic.

<h1 style="text-align:center">24</h1>

THE weather had changed and become sunny and warm. April with its sudden showers and uncertain skies had given way to the first day of May. In the hall at Dashbury the barometer was tapped and consulted. The fountain was turned on and Neptune, slimy with falling water, threw a sparkling shower into the air through a concealed lead pipe inserted in the conch shell which he held in his hands. Lilacs beyond the formal garden and near the house came out and their scent filled the air. Soft white balls of guelder roses hung motionless in the windless air. The kitchen garden blossomed with starry flowers and the scene was set for a sort of splendour of beauty which only comes late in April and early May where blossom and scent are apt to be scattered by scuds of rain and chivvying winds.

Lucy had won a grudging assent to go down to the library and help George, only given because Ada knew that Hugh would consider Lucy's help there more important than her own work and would be displeased if that help was withheld.

Violet was having breakfast upstairs when Lucy came down timidly into the library. She found Ludovic there with George. Both men seemed pleased to see her and she was soon seated at the big writing table copying down the names and dates of books in her neat, round handwriting. Ludovic prowled about, taking out a book here and there and whistling a little tune to himself, while George appeared to be absorbed in each volume that he carefully scrutinised.

Some time later the door opened and Violet came in, her face alight with curiosity and looking as if she was seeking some form of mischief.

"You all look very busy and solemn," she said. "May I come in?"

Lucy rose to her feet, George closed the stout volume he was holding and Ludovic spun round, his face alight.

"Good morning," said Violet, "you are all very busy. I mustn't interrupt, must I?"

"Let's go for a walk," said Ludovic, "and leave George and Lucy at their labours."

Violet looked at Ludovic, then at George. She ignored Lucy. "Couldn't I help?" she asked, going up to a shelf and looking at the books.

George stared at her and Ludovic said, "No, come out, Violet. It's too good a morning to spend indoors. We'll leave George and Lucy to get on with their work."

As he went out with Violet she cast a glance back into the library. Lucy had sat down and George had taken another book out of the shelves.

"Should you not be out this fine morning, Miss Lucy?" said George.

Lucy looked up, surprised. "No, I never go out in the mornings," she said. "I have to do things in the house."

"I see. Well, if you will, just make a note of this," and he read out the name and description of the book, bound in flaking leather, and then brought it over to the table for Lucy to look at. Lucy looked at it and carefully noted all the idiosyncrasies of the title page, while George went back to the bookshelf and found another book to study. The library was silent except for the loud ticking of the clock. The two people in it exchanged few words and George felt the pleasantness and peace of working with Lucy.

In his life of hard work and accurate study as a don women had played very little part. Apart from a short-lived fancy for a bright-eyed young cousin in Scotland whom he soon got over and quickly forgot when she married and left to live in Edinburgh, his life had been lived a little aridly and without any desire for a wife or family. Something now stirred in his mind—the possibility of happiness, of a life with a companion whose response to his work would be eager, and who would bring a softness and gentleness into his life. This life at Oxford, as he stood book in hand, seemed to be completely lacking in these qualities. At that moment Lucy looked up at him and smiled.

After a little time of waiting, Ludovic went out on to the terrace through the french windows. Violet emerged, complete with hat and cape, and they set off down to the steps to the fountain. Violet glanced sideways at Ludovic, wondering how easily she could make him lose his head and fall in love with her. She had known every move in the game ever since she was a child of fourteen, with a mane of chestnut-coloured hair and vivid pink in her cheeks. She knew how to coax and bring on and hold back and hoodwink anyone who she wished to further her pleasures and ambitions. Married to man older than herself by ten years she had brought a gaiety and sense of fun into his rather dull and formal life. Of course she didn't tell him everything; after all he wouldn't understand about all the things she wanted to do or what it was like to be brilliant and lovely and sought after, though Henry's pride in her loveliness and charm was, she thought, inexhaustible. Sometimes, however, a creeping doubt had assailed her in the last year. Henry had once or twice looked at her with surprise and with a look in his eyes that showed a sort of puzzled doubt about a careless statement that failed to square with something she had told him the week before. Dear Henry, she thought. She had been brought up by a strictly religious mother to stick to the letter of the truth, but for truth in the abstract Violet had little use and no interest. She had spent her life slipping round corners, real or imaginary, by serving out a measure of fantasy and fact. Her statements, which were profusely overlaid with charm and cajolery, usually enveloped her family and friends in a mesh of bewilderment, and had not seldom made them feel, when the tears sprang to her eyes, that they had hurt and misunderstood dear little Violet, and that in some obscure way they were guilty of unkindness.

But all this was far removed from Violet's thoughts this morning as she sat on the edge of the fountain with an attractive young man. Ludovic looked at the house, mellow and gracious against the shining sky, and listened to the birds singing with a sense of a late spring. Violet was a Londoner by preference and the country sights and sounds were either pleasant or tiresome—tiresome because of the rain which spoiled a garden party, or pleasant when they made a suitable setting for her as on an occasion like this.

They talked of mutual acquaintances, Violet feeling her way. She had a gift for description of people and things which was shrewd and amusing and occasionally a streak of malice peeped out like the sudden emergence of claws from underneath the velvet paws of a cat, which Violet's detractors said she resembled with her widely set eyes, her purring voice and coaxing ways.

"Lady Ashendon and Mr. Ludovic are in the garden, m'lady," announced Soey from the window.

Jane Dashbury moved restlessly in her chair. Soey stood at the window until Violet rose and with Ludovic walked away towards the tangle of bushes and flowering trees and disappeared under the archway.

Ludovic felt enchantment closing round him. He gave a side glance at his companion's lovely profile as they paced together through the artificial tunnel with light at the end. Could this be England, could it be Dashbury, this place which he connected with a great deal of cold fog and a vast amount of boredom?

Ludovic did most of the talking while Violet listened to all that he was saying with beguiling attention. She had all the attributes of a good listener and a gift for remembering afterwards what she had heard; even those who were not greatly moved by her beauty always wished to meet her again, as they had found someone who appeared to have no interest in the world except their likes and dislikes, their troubles, disagreements and disappointments. Ludovic, who was usually more of a listener than a talker, found himself telling her of his life in Rome and his devotion to Italy.

Violet listened, smiled, and somehow conveyed a shaft of warmer interest in the tone of her voice under her light words. Then she glanced at the small watch which, backed by a diamond cypher on a gold background, was hanging round her neck. She put her hand lightly on to Ludovic's arm.

"I think I must go now," she said, "and see Aunt Louise and perhaps old Lady Dashbury. You know I would rather, much rather, continue our walk."

They retraced their steps and mounted the terrace to the house. "I must take a peep at the library and see what your friend and Lucy are doing," she said, as she softly approached the window. As she looked through it they saw Lucy still seated at the large writing table, her chin in her hand and George standing by her with an open book. He was smiling as he looked down at her upturned face. They were both so intent on what they were saying to each other that they didn't notice for a moment the two figures outside the window. George looked up and saw them and Lucy turned her head.

"I must go," said Violet, and walked away to the french windows of the drawing-room. Ludovic followed her but did not see a slight tightening of her lips and an expression on her face which he could not have interpreted.

Violet was conducted upstairs by Louise to see Jane Dashbury. Soey had wrapped the whitest and fleeciest shawl she could find round her mistress's shoulders and Jane surveyed her visitor from a background of white linen and pearly lace.

She enquired after Violet's husband and child and listened in silence while Violet told her that dear Henry was well; but the poor dear was always busy, what with estate business and then, of course, the House of Lords and racing, and all the other things he had to do, and what with the exigencies of social life she did not see as much of him as she wished. And then little Henry, he was already two years old and beginning to lisp a few words and sometimes for a moment looked just a little like his Aunt Louise and her side of the family, which was so nice, and it was so delightful to be back in lovely Dashbury. She always enjoyed her visits there so much, and this time such beautiful weather. The whole place was like an enchanting fairy tale. And how was she, dear Lady Dashbury?

"About the same as usual," answered Jane. "I am hoping to go back to the Dower House soon. How do you find your Aunt Louise?"

Violet hesitated for a moment, and said that Aunt Louise seemed well but a little depressed, she thought.

Violet's eyes were fixed on the carpet at her feet and she suddenly lifted them and looked at Jane. There might or might not have been a meaning in her glance. Jane returned her look with steady composure. "Everyone gets depressed at times," she said. "The task of directing a very big household like this is not easy and it becomes monotonous. I will speak to Hugh about it. He may not wish to have the expense of opening the house in London, but we must see what can be done. When I move to the Dower House Ada could go to London."

"And Lucy?"

"Oh, Lucy can come with me. I shall be very glad to have her company. This house can always be half shut up. Hugh is returning tomorrow and no doubt he will tell us about his decision."

"Dear Uncle Hugh, it will be nice to see him," murmured Violet.

"He will be delighted to see you," said Jane, "and hear of all Henry's doings," and with these two brief politenesses Violet took her leave and the luncheon gong sounded throughout the house.

25

"You must go out of doors, Mr. Maxwell," said Louise at luncheon. "You really cannot work at books all day."

"I'm very well used to doing so," he replied. "But," he added, "after tea I should like to go for a walk; perhaps

Miss Lucy would show me where the Pleasure Ground is. I understand that it is worth seeing and commands a good view of the house."

If George had thrown a fire-cracker on to the table the effect could not have been more instantaneous.

Lucy's face coloured, Louise looked surprised, and Ludovic and Violet stopped their exchange of light talk.

Louise remarked: "Certainly the evenings are drawing out, but the Pleasure Ground is not at its best at the moment as the rhododendrons are not out. But the bluebells are lovely under the trees."

"Well, then, I shall look forward to my walk," said George. "Will you come, Miss Lucy?"

"Of course she'll come," said Ludovic. "I can't imagine a better guide than Lucy. She often walks there and knows all the places from which you can see the best views of the house."

After tea George and Lucy went out together.

"I must say . . ." began Ada.

"Let's go out too," said Ludovic to Violet, springing to his feet. Ada and Louise were left alone.

Ada's foot tapped on the ground and she rubbed her hands together. "I must say," she repeated, "I can't imagine why you and Hugh encourage Lucy to be with that man so much." Louise, who was examining her rings, looked at her sister-in-law. Her mind was obviously a long way away on some errand of its own.

"What man?" she asked. "Oh, I see, you mean Mr. Maxwell. I don't know what you're saying, Ada, about encouraging him. Hugh wants Lucy to help him by writing out the titles of the books. It saves time and why shouldn't she go for a walk with him?"

"He might be taking a fancy to her."

Louise opened her eyes widely. "I think it's most

unlikely. Lucy is not the sort of girl men take fancies to very much. Besides," she added, "if he did it would be quite a suitable match for her. Hugh tells me he belongs to a good Scotch family."

Ada bounced in her seat. "But I couldn't spare Lucy," she said, "I've too much work in hand, and I daresay you would miss her a lot too. After all, she runs a great many errands for you in the day."

"Yes," agreed Louise, "but I might get someone else perhaps. Rhoda might come for a little. She's been far more in society than Lucy and she could do a great deal to help me with my clothes and so on."

"She wouldn't help me," said Ada angrily.

"No, I suppose not," said her sister-in-law languidly.

Ada sat frowning and angry. She detested Rhoda, who was a cousin of Louise's, and regarded her as an empty-headed and fashionable butterfly.

Ada left the room and Louise smiled to herself as she rose and looked out of the window.

Lucy and George started their walk ascending a broad grass track. George broke the silence by remarking that he thought he had done a good day's work on the books. Lucy looked up with her face alight with pleasure. "I should like to show you some of the Oxford libraries," he continued.

A cuckoo's call came from the wood above them. Its wild, irresponsible gaiety echoed all over the valley and menaced the domesticity and comfort of the nesting birds.

"I should like to see those libraries," said Lucy.

They had reached the iron gate and mounting some steps found themselves in the Pleasure Ground, with a small sheet of water in front of them. The rhododendron bushes came down to its edge and the so-called temple, with Doric columns supporting a slate-grey roof, looked shadowy and mysterious. The tall trees which backed the little building and the sheet of water below it were peaceable and withdrawn, and made a charming place for rambling walks and solitary meditation.

Lucy and George waited for a moment listening to the calling of the birds, the soft rustling of small animals in the bushes and the gentle wind stirring the tree-tops. By mutual consent they were silent as they moved slowly along a grass-grown path which led to the temple. Silently they sat down and looked over at the house below them. Neither of them spoke, until George said: "This place is very beautiful this evening. Oxford is lovely too this time of year. This is its blossoming time. Will you come there some time, Miss Lucy? I'll take you on the river."

"If I can," she said, her heart beating. To see Oxford, and to be asked in such a way! "I've never been away since I came here." She looked up at him. "I would like to go if I can—I mean, if it's possible."

"Ludovic could make it possible," George replied. "I must speak to him."

George's words added the last touch of perfection to the evening. She looked up at him and their eyes met.

The rhododendron bushes near them shook and crackled.

"Oh, there you are!" cried Violet. "Ludovic and I came to find you. We thought we saw you from the other side of the water, but you were talking so hard we couldn't attract your attention."

George looked at Violet with surprise. His quietly spaced words to Lucy could hardly be described as talking hard.

"Move along, Lucy," said Violet, "we would like to sit down and look at the view too."

Lucy moved to the end of the seat and sat on its edge. Violet sat down and fanned herself with her handkerchief. She looked flushed and laughing. Ludovic did not look sulky, but quite pleased, and George sat in silence. The scene was as enchanting as before, but the enchantment for Lucy had vanished. It had become reduced to a sheet of water, bushes and the wood, a small stone building and a house in a valley.

Violet seemed unconscious of being the cause of any disturbance, and directed laughing glances at the two men.

"Have you enjoyed your walk after your long day's work?" she said, turning to George.

"I've very much enjoyed my walk."

"I expect you and Lucy talk about nothing but books," she said. "Lucy's bookish. Do you like bookish women, Mr. Maxwell?"

"I like to talk to anyone who loves books," said George. "And Miss Lucy loves them."

'Is he going to say that he's asked me to come to Oxford?' thought Lucy, her hand tightly gripping the edge of the seat. But George said nothing more; he turned to Ludovic and asked him a question about the Pleasure Ground. Ludovic replied that it had been laid out by the Dashbury who built the house, and whose wife had indulged in violent tempers. He made the Pleasure Ground so that he could escape and sit in the temple and meditate and be at peace with a book. "There is skating here in the winter," said Ludovic. "The pond keeps frozen far longer than most bits of water owing to being so sheltered by trees and bushes."

Violet pouted a little. She liked conversation to be personal, and history and memories filled her with *ennui*.

"I must be getting back," said Lucy.

Ludovic rose. "We'd all better go back," he said.

"Yes, I expect we ought to," said Violet, "or we shall be late for dinner."

They went in Indian file between the bushes. The birds had stopped calling to each other and there was the hush of approaching evening. In the valley smoke rose straight from the chimneys of the house in the still air.

'She spoils everything,' thought Lucy, 'we were so happy, at least I was,' and so she thought was George.

Violet and Lucy passed first through the gate. Ludovic stopped for a moment to fasten its catch, and Violet, addressing a remark to George, walked down the hill with him.

Ludovic walked beside Lucy, switching the head off a flower with his cane. He was frowning.

"When is Uncle Hugh coming, Lucy?" he asked in order to break the silence. He frowned impatiently when she said "Tomorrow, I think." Ludovic was clearly not looking forward to a meeting with his uncle. He looked cross and was oblivious to the loveliness of the scene before them.

Lucy looked at Violet's elegant back and her uplifted profile as she talked to George, who bent his head to listen. He seemed to be smiling down at her.

Lucy went straight downstairs, encountering no one on the stairs. Her mind was in a turmoil. When George had suggested her going to Oxford and there had been a moment when something, an inflection in his voice, in a moment's crystallisation of beauty and poetry, there had been a hope of a remote dream come true. It had ended abruptly as dreams so often do, but perhaps ...

Ludovic's temper had not improved by dinner. Violet exerted herself to keep the conversation going. She drew Louise and Ada into the net of her talk; she directed challenging glances at Ludovic, and threw a word and an occasional glance at Lucy.

After dinner Louise walked to the fireplace and warmed her hands. The evening had grown colder. Then she looked up at the mantelpiece and took down two octagonal-shaped hand screens and called to Ada to look at them.

Violet and Ludovic had walked to the other end of the room. Lucy stood by the card table, lifting a pack of cards and letting them slide slowly through her fingers.

She turned her head and saw Violet put her hand on Ludovic's arm; then, before she could look away, she saw Ludovic give a quick glance at his two aunts then put his hand over Violet's.

"Why are you so cross?" she heard Violet saying, directing a melting glance at him.

"You know quite well." And then Louise called to her and Lucy turned away.

Louise pointed out that one of the little screens wanted mending and asked Lucy to see to it.

George had gone back to the library to put in an extra hour's work and the rest of the party converged on the card table and sat down to a round game.

George reappeared just as they had finished it and apologised for having been so long away. He came and stood behind Lucy's chair. As she looked up at him he asked her if she would give him some help the following morning.

"What is this wonderful help Lucy gives you? Does she dust the books for you, or what?" said Violet.

"She does a great deal more than that," said George. "She has a real understanding of what I am doing."

There was a moment's silence and Louise remarked, "I'm sure Lucy does all she can to help. Just deal the cards round once more, Ludovic, then we must go to bed."

When Violet retired to her room, she looked at herself for some time in the mirror on her dressing table. This usually gave her a vast amount of satisfaction. She adjusted a curl of hair and examined her face in case a faint line might have become visible on her forehead. There was no line and the curls were just as shining and lustrous as ever, but she was not entirely satisfied. She bit her lips and suddenly felt years older than Ludovic though there was only a year between them. She rose and paced the room. Ludovic should have known all the rules of the game of flirtation. He had lived abroad in foreign capitals, notorious hotbeds of intrigue and gaiety of all kinds. An expert on the subject of flirtation at the age of fourteen, Violet knew exactly how far she was prepared to go, and she had a great deal of experience in preventing any scandal being made by those who had misinterpreted the warmth of her interest towards them. She was attracted by Ludovic. He was so charming and good-looking, and she loved admiration. His talk and even his compliments were slightly edged with irony which made him a more stimulating companion than the men she was accustomed to meeting.

Violet loved playing with fire and she excused herself by saying to herself that dear Henry was so good and upright, and that he would make allowances for her youth and wish to be gay. Somewhere in the back of her mind she knew that she had come across something inflexible in Henry, a stubbornness that was really regrettable, as after all she was only young, and youth did not last but gave place to years of enforced and dreary respectability stretching into the future. She shivered and pulled her dressing-gown more closely round her. George Maxwell, too, she couldn't leave him alone. His aloofness piqued her and his austere looks were a challenge. He was, she had an idea, attracted to Lucy. Well, that didn't matter, it should be easy to dazzle him. No one would look at Lucy while she was there. The moon would easily be extinguished by the full blaze of the sun. That Lucy had a quiet sort of charm she was not capable of seeing or of understanding. She dismissed Lucy from her mind. An uncomfortable stirring on the part of her usually quiescent conscience reminded her that Lucy might not have many chances of marriage and it was unfair to try to spoil perhaps the only one she would have. As Violet climbed into the fourposter bed, she remarked to herself, "I'm sure she could find a curate to marry somewhere around here."

26

GEORGE and LUCY were left undisturbed in the library for most of the next morning. The skies had remained cloudless and Ludovic had asked Louise if he could take Violet for a drive in the phaeton. Louise had agreed to this with outward politeness but with inward misgivings. Louise knew that Hugh would be disagreeably surprised that her niece was conducting such an open flirtation with his nephew, but she could not think rapidly enough to give any reason to refuse.

Ludovic had in the last week gone, it seemed to her, beyond anyone's control. He had lost his head over Violet like many another young man.

Lucy looked at Ludovic, mutely hoping that he had some idea where he was going. Her mind was in a turmoil for George dominated her thoughts. But she had become very fond of Ludovic and she had looked forward to his return and the pleasantness of having a companion of her own age who in his own way was so kind and thoughtful.

The splendour of the late spring with its attendant scenes and flowers made a pagan setting to the pagan splendour of the house. Violet's disturbing presence made for excitement but an inward disquiet. No one was at ease.

Even Bourton's looks had a latent anxiety as he presided over the footmen at meals.

The only room in the house where Lucy felt at all at peace was Jane Dashbury's bedroom. She lay under her window which fronted on to the park, letting the soft breeze blow fitfully on to her face and faintly stir the lace lapels of her cap. Soey, still fortified by the saying 'Ne'er cast a clout till May is out', remained in her fusty black alpaca garments. She reminded everyone of the near presence of winter, and of the folly of giving the English climate an inch lest it should take an ell.

Jane looked a little firmer and less transparent in the face, but her eyes were disturbed and she looked less serene, although she put no anxiety into words.

Violet had visited her for short talks with an air of doing a pleasurable duty, but she had seen very little of her and Ludovic only briefly. At the moment he was an unsatisfactory companion.

Jane was much too wise to try and keep him long with her, for though love and duty kept him sitting talking to her his mind was bubbling over with heady thoughts and his body seemed strung to concert pitch.

George Maxwell also came to see her. He left his sentences unfinished, which was completely out of character with him, and altogether Jane Dashbury wished ardently that the workmen had departed so that she could be moved to the Dower House and resume the quiet tenor of her days there. At other moments she had a longing to be well and strong again and go downstairs and see things for herself. Soey contented herself with hints: "There's Mr. Ludovic in the garden again," she would remark. "Out with her ladyship, Miss Violet that was. They've gone out in the phaeton again to Dashbury. Miss Brown, Miss Violet's maid, is going to show me her wardrobe this afternoon. They say that she has more than twenty dresses and six parasols and thirty pairs of shoes. Miss Lucy should take a tonic, m'lady, she doesn't look well."

Jane listened without one word, with outward calm but inward anxiety, to Soey's remarks. With all her devotion to her mistress, Soey could make statements which were disturbing to her and made her unhappy.

One morning Louise remarked, "I have had a letter from Theresa Wilson Fyfield. She is driving over today with Katharine."

"Oh," said Violet, "I know Theresa. She's a cousin of my father's."

Violet conveyed by the tone of her voice that this gave her no pleasure. "I don't want to see her, gossipy old cat," she said afterwards to Ludovic. "Why does Aunt Louise let her come?"

Ludovic frowned. "Well, I suppose she can't very well say no. They're neighbours. I don't think that anyone wants to see her. Aunt Ada can't bear her."

"What's Katharine like?"

"I hardly know her," said Ludovic, adding, "Well, we might manage to be late for tea."

"That won't do. They'll only say that I did it on purpose to be out with you. She'll tell all my relations that. No, we must come into tea, very prim and proper, by separate doors. Aunt Louise can entertain them herself, she has let them come. Lucy and your speechless professor won't be much help."

"George isn't speechless at all," said Ludovic in a tone of sharpness. "It's that he only talks if he has something to say that is worth saying."

"What on earth would society be like if we all did that?" said Violet. "There would be no conversation at all. As a matter of fact he does talk to me when no one else is there.

I went into the library and I assure you we had a nice long talk."

"Was Lucy there?"

"No, she was not. She left the room when I came in."

"For God's sake, Violet, leave George alone. All you'll do is to spoil his friendship with Lucy, and then you'll go away and forget all about him."

Violet put her hand on his arm. "Ludovic dear," she said, looking up to him, "I'm not thinking of any man but you, and, of course, dear Henry."

"Damn Henry!" said Ludovic under his breath.

"Ludovic!" cried Violet in a shocked tone, but jealousy in a man was meat and drink to her. "Henry is my husband," she said smoothly.

"Do you think I don't know that? Heavens, I know that. Look, I must talk to you. We must talk. We never seem to be more than a short time together in this house. People are always coming in or out and in the garden Mundell or one of his gardeners are there."

"Well, let's go for a drive this afternoon."

"Yes, but I can't talk to you when we're driving."

However, they set out for their drive—"Just a very short one, Aunt Louise, only round the park."

"Well, don't be long," said Louise. She looked preoccupied as she turned to Lucy and gave her a message for the still-room.

George was leaving the following day, and Lucy looked at the pile of books on the table with a pang.

"I will just look through them before putting them back on the shelves, and put everything straight. Lord Dashbury is very kindly allowing me to take some books on my own subject back to Oxford. If you could copy a list of them while I have one more look round, I shall be very grateful."

Lucy took up her pen and inscribed names and particulars of books in silence. George wandered round the library, taking books out and replacing them in a desultory way unlike his usual purposeful method of working. "Miss Lucy," he said suddenly, and Lucy started and put down her pen. The last few days had been such unhappy ones. She had sat by and seen Violet trying her seductive glances on George and asking him questions about Oxford and listening, finger pressed into her cheek, with flattering attention; coming into the library when George and she were at work, introducing an element of disruption and idleness, with Ludovic frowning and irritable behind her. He had spoken very little to Lucy during his visit and Lucy had a pang of regret that a friend had turned away from her, as well as a deeper and more poignant anxiety.

She trembled a little, laid down her pen, and tried to occupy herself with the paper on the table; but it rattled in her hands, which shook a little.

"Miss Lucy," he said again, and clasped his hands together as his agitation seemed to match hers. "I hope you will come to Oxford. I would much like it if you would. I should greatly like to show you my college and my study."

Lucy looked up at him. "I should love to come," she said, "but I don't know if I can."

"Perhaps Ludovic could bring you. Or can't you count on him?"

She shook her head. "Not at the moment, I can't," she said. She hadn't meant to say this, but the words were forced from her.

"He's quite infatuated, you mean. I cannot myself get a word of sense from him. I don't know when this is going to end, or where it will lead. Ludovic has always been on the whole a person of sense and balance. At the moment there's no hope for him. But I have some friends in London;

he is Scotch and a barrister, and they would travel down with you and bring you back to London. It would, I know, please them if you would stay a night with them before returning here."

Lucy's face lit up and she had a momentary loveliness, which comes from unhappiness being turned into joy, winter going and spring coming.

George looked down at her. "If you will come to Oxford," he said, "we can perhaps talk . . ." he hesitated, "about the future. I have something to say to you . . . something. When I leave tomorrow I shall write to you if I may."

Lucy bowed her head and said "Yes."

"I should say it now but this place oppresses me. Although it is so large there is no privacy. Someone always looks in and interrupts."

At that moment the door opened and Ludovic came in. "You seem very busy, you two," he said.

"We're finishing the work," said George drily, "as I am leaving by tomorrow's train."

"Well, can I help?" said Ludovic.

"Yes, you can. You can explain anything I haven't made clear. I can show you my notes," and he handed Ludovic a sheaf of papers. Ludovic sat and appeared to peruse them, but it was clear that his mind was elsewhere. He frowned, crossed and uncrossed his legs, fidgeted, and asked one or two questions then stared out of the window.

George looked impartially at him, replying to his questions, and went on explaining and rearranging books, a frown on his face.

'Violet's ruining their friendship,' thought Lucy confusedly.

The two men talked together and Ludovic was obviously trying to give his mind to the matter in hand. He brought over a page to Lucy. "What did you mean by this word?" he asked.

Lucy said, "I'm sorry, the pen slipped. I should have corrected it."

"Oh, don't bother. Just correct it now. It's only happened once. You write so clearly as a rule."

Later Violet and Ludovic went out for a drive, while Louise awaited Mrs. Wilson Fyfield and Katharine in the drawing-room. Louise had asked Jane Dashbury if she would like to see Theresa Fyfield, and Jane, though tired and in pain, said that she would.

"You're sure it will not be too much for you? I'm glad you will see her. That voice of hers gets on my nerves."

"Oh, I'm delighted to help. I don't suppose she can stay long."

"Well, she will always stay on and on, but I will send Lucy up to bring her downstairs after about twenty minutes."

"I can bear Theresa for half an hour, I think."

Lucy was in the drawing-room with Louise when the visitors arrived.

Theresa advanced saying: "I felt I must see you all before we go to London for the season."

Katharine followed her slowly. Her glance and Lucy's met. Mrs. Wilson Fyfield's glance swept the room and the table prepared for tea. The two ladies seated themselves on a sofa in the window, while Lucy and Katharine went out on to the terrace. Mrs. Wilson Fyfield enquired after the health of the whole family.

"Ludovic is staying here and my niece Violet Ashendon, and Mr. Maxwell, Ludovic's Oxford friend, who is leaving tomorrow."

Mrs. Fyfield started at the mention of Violet.

"I didn't know she was here."

"She always comes to us for a yearly visit."

"How is she? I heard she was losing her looks a little."

"I haven't seen any sign of that. She is out at the moment. Ludovic's taken her for a drive, they will be back for tea."

Mrs. Wilson Fyfield first looked startled and then displeased. Thrown off her guard, she plucked crossly at her ample skirt with her gloved hand.

"Do you think it wise, Louise," she said angrily, "to let Ludovic go about with a married woman? And surely you and Hugh wish to see him suitably married to a nice girl?"

Louise, although unobservant of other people's feelings, was beginning to be extremely uneasy over Ludovic's preoccupation with Violet, and replied in a slightly defensive tone: "Violet happens to be staying here and so does Ludovic. I cannot prevent them seeing a great deal of each other."

At that moment Bourton and a footman brought in the tea and Lucy and Katharine came in through the french windows. In the light spring dress she was wearing Katharine looked charming and carried herself with more confidence.

"I think we'd better have tea," said Louise.

Katharine had been puzzled in the few minutes she had had alone with Lucy, partly by her look of happiness and partly by the shadow which came over her face when she talked of Ludovic. She took her place near Lucy, leaving a vacant chair between them and the older ladies.

Mrs. Fyfield had swallowed her vexation with her first cup of tea and was smiling graciously. When the door opened and Ludovic came in, he looked flushed and apologetic. One of the ponies in the phaeton had cast a shoe and they had had to drive home at a very slow pace. Violet was coming along in a moment.

Louise received his apologies without a word. She was put out and showed it. Mrs. Wilson Fyfield, on the other hand, gave him her hand with effusion, and smiled at him with her head cocked on one side. He seated himself by her side.

"You haven't been over to see us. The General and I have been expecting you, and so has Katharine."

Katharine, embarrassed, sat at a loss. Ludovic was preparing to make some kind of reply when Violet came in. She advanced full of charming apologies, but showed no real discomposure. A stranger, seeing her greetings to Theresa, would have assumed that they were full of delight at seeing each other. They exclaimed with pleasure, Violet enquired after General Fyfield and Mrs. Fyfield after Henry and the little boy and Violet's parents. Ludovic, who knew of Violet's dislike of Theresa, and what Theresa thought of Violet, managed composure with difficulty. Lucy and Katharine, who had by now drunk their tea, sat in silence, and Ludovic, as he turned from Theresa to Katharine, was conscious of a disturbing embarrassment when he met her steady grey eyes.

In the last two months Katharine had grown up. Helped by Lucy, she had embarked on a steady course of reading. She had quietly asked for and obtained from her father a share of the money left by her mother as a dress allowance; her clothes had now improved and had a look both of simplicity and fashion. Her secret thoughts about Ludovic she confided to no one; although Lucy suspected, they never spoke of them.

Although Ludovic studiously averted his eyes from Violet, and Violet was much too astute to parade a conquest in front of a malicious gossip like Theresa Fyfield, undercurrents of excitement ran beneath the placid waters of the country-house tea-party. Katharine appeared unaware of it and composedly asked Ludovic about his work at the Embassy in Rome, and listened with interest to his replies. She enquired whether the Colosseum by moonlight was as fine as it was described to be, and Ludovic replied that if anything it was finer than any description. Theresa, determined to keep Ludovic talking to Katharine, plunged into a forecast of the gaieties of the forthcoming London season, and Violet was entangled in answering questions and making comments and listening to surmises. Louise listened, putting in a word here and there, and Lucy sat on, wondering and looking.

At last Louise said to Theresa, "Shall we go for a turn on the terrace?"

The drawing-room seemed to have become intolerably heated by the cross currents of talk, and a gratefully cool breeze circled round them as they stepped out of sight. Lucy was the only one of the party who derived any pleasure from the evening scene. It was that hour before twilight begins, when the only sound came from the splashing of the fountain and the calls of the blackbirds running in and out of the shrubberies. Louise suddenly remembered the fact that Theresa was due to visit her mother-in-law, and with her came back into the house. They mounted the stairs together in almost complete silence.

The four young people descended the steps of the fountain. Violet seated herself on the stone rim and splashed her hand in the water. "Lucy," she said, "do please go and get some crumbs for the goldfish. I always feed them."

Lucy complied, went back into the drawing-room and taking a bun from the plate on the depleted tea table, retraced her steps down to the fountain.

She paused on the steps of the terrace. Katharine was sitting on the stone kerb beside the fountain, her head was bent and her slim hands clasped round her knees. Violet was looking up at Ludovic with a laughing glance. He seemed a little ill at ease as he stood with his hands in his pockets looking at her.

Lucy handed the bun to Violet, who crumbled it, and the fish, dull gold and green, rushed to get to it. As they looked down into the water Katharine stood up and slipped her hand through Lucy's arm.

"Let's go for a stroll," she said, and they went away together under the arched walk.

"Don't let's talk," said Katharine as they passed along the mossy path.

"No. We won't talk. We won't say a word," said Lucy.

They sat down on a stone seat which was rickety and old and crumbling. It commanded a small vista of path and shrubs and in a few moments Katharine stared and looked down at the ground.

Lucy was afraid of tears and swollen eyelids and pale cheeks, but Katharine sat silent and dry-eyed. Lucy sat quite still and listened to the rustling of the small animals in the bushes.

Meanwhile, Violet threw crumbs to the fishes. After a pause she remarked, "I suppose that's the girl they all want you to marry."

Ludovic flushed. "Nobody's got any idea of such a thing," he said.

"Oh, haven't they?" said Violet with a little laugh. "That's where you're mistaken, my dear boy. I've heard rumours of it. Theresa thinks you're a catch in the matrimonial market, with a future title and this place," and she waved her hand towards the house and the further scene of fairy wood and Pleasure Ground where the temple showed between the trees.

"Violet," said Ludovic, "this is vulgar."

148

"Of course it is," said Violet calmly. "Society is vulgar, and so is Theresa."

"I don't want this place or the title or the money."

"Well, never mind." Violet dusted her hands together. "Don't get cross. I hate people to get cross. It's such a lovely evening. Let's go back to the house."

As they mounted the terrace steps Violet said over her shoulder, "My dear, that girl would make a very presentable Lady Dashbury if she was more smartly dressed. She seems a nice enough girl, too." With that she disappeared through the french window, walked rapidly across the drawing-room, and was gone.

Ludovic kicked a footstool savagely out of his way and muttered something under his breath.

"I shall come back in ten minutes," Louise said, after Jane Dashbury had greeted Theresa.

Theresa smoothed her gloves and fidgeted with her reticule. She looked ruffled and cross. Jane, though tired by pain and exhausted by Theresa's conversation, ignored a passing hint about Ludovic and Violet, smiled and tried to bring the conversation on to a calm, even level; but it was not easy to converse with Theresa, who resembled a smouldering volcano. Theresa answered the questions about the General and their plans for the London season curtly, and finally burst forth with: "Violet's at her tricks again. I must say that for a married woman she is behaving outrageously, and Ludovic seems quite taken by her. I don't know what Louise is thinking about, having them here together, but of course Louise wouldn't mind. She . . ."

"Theresa, would you just call my maid to bring me my smelling salts?" said Jane, closing her eyes.

Theresa, a good deal alarmed, summoned Soey, who was

caught in the act of observing Ludovic and Violet in conversation by the fountain. She dropped the curtains she had drawn aside with a start and bustled into the room with restoratives.

Jane opened her eyes, smiled at Theresa. "I'm better now," she said. "No, do sit down again, it's only a passing faintness." But at that moment Louise came in.

On the doorstep under the pillared porch there was an outwardly attractive scene of family farewells. Violet and Theresa took leave of each other with protestations of how much they looked forward to seeing each other in London. Theresa made voluble apologies for having tired Jane to Louise. Lucy and Katharine gave each other an almost wordless goodbye—"We will meet before we go to London," Katharine whispered in Lucy's ear as they embraced on the edge of the group. Katharine looked steadily at Ludovic as she said goodbye, shook hands with Violet and followed her stepmother into the waiting carriage.

Lucy ran upstairs to Jane Dashbury's room. "Did Mrs. Fyfield upset you? How are you feeling?"

Jane's colour had returned to her face. "A weak heart can be a very useful thing at times, my dear," she said, "from every point of view."

"You mean . . ." said Lucy, staring at her.

"I mean exactly what I say," replied Jane.

George had left the afternoon before and Ada had gone by the same train. Neither looked forward to the journey together. Ada had announced with an air of mystery and importance that she had plans she must make in London. George resolved to bury his head in a book the moment the train left Dashbury station.

Hugh Dashbury had announced his intention of returning from London the day after the Fyfield visit. Violet had no doubt that when Uncle Hugh came back an air of decorum would be imposed on the whole household. She chose her simplest dress to wear in the evening. He had come by late train and arrived just before dinner, and as she came into the room she saw him standing there. It struck her that he looked tired and haggard, and the lines on his face had deepened.

As he came forward to meet her, he gave her a sharp glance. He was one of the few men of Violet's acquaintance whom she'd never been able to charm. He admired her looks but was disturbed when she married his friend Henry Ashendon, for whom he had a warm respect and liking. The whispers which had reached him about Violet's flirtations had caused him nothing but a growing disapproval. He enquired after her parents, her husband, and her son, and then offered her his arm. Violet had more than a nodding acquaintance with politics and the affairs of the great world and was adept at concealing the shallowness of her knowledge. She asked Hugh a question and followed it up by such a demure show of interest that all the rest of the family seated round the table felt their interest also stirred. Violet listened with an air of rapt interest while Hugh was talking and led him to further talk by a well-placed question or interjection.

After dinner Hugh refused a game of whist saying that he should go to bed and try and sleep off his fatigue. Louise followed him into the hall to make some arrangements for the next day. Lucy left the room by another door to enquire from Soey whether Jane Dashbury was feeling better. Soey replied that Jane had just gone off to sleep and Lucy, after fetching her work from her bedroom, returned to the drawing-room. Ludovic and Violet were talking earnestly by the fire. They separated and Violet sat down at the card table and laid out the cards for patience. Louise returned and brought out some needlework and she and Lucy sat opposite each other while Violet and Ludovic played a game. They presented the spectacle of two cousins amicably engaged in a two-handed patience, but as Lucy drew her needle in and out she felt a mounting tension between them. It showed in the glances that Violet gave Ludovic as she deliberately chose a red card to put on to a black one, her rings sparkling on the whiteness of her hands.

When Louise folded up her work and announced that it had been a tiring day and that they had all better go to bed, Violet patted back a yawn and the three ladies filed out of the dark hall where Ludovic lighted the silver candlesticks. They parted at their bedroom doors. Violet was yawning again, though smiling at her aunt.

The house was still and rather airless when Violet opened her bedroom door and, candlestick in hand, peeped cautiously out into the passage. Silently and lightly, clasping the candlestick in one hand and her long skirt in the other, she went softly down into the dark well of the hall and as softly opened the drawing-room door, closing it soundlessly behind her. Two lamps were burning on tables and there was a thin scent of paraffin in the air as if they'd been freshly lit. Ludovic was in the act of turning up the wick of one of them.

"At last," he said, "we can talk. We've had so little of it since you came, Violet. I am so thankful to see you."

"I can't stay, I daren't."

"It's all right, everybody's in bed, and tomorrow there'll be no chance of anything with Uncle Hugh here. Violet, dearest darling, I love you, you know I do."

"No, Ludovic, you mustn't say that."

He sat down by her. "But I must tell you, I will. I can't keep silent any longer. You must have seen, I know you have seen, that I have been falling deeper and deeper in love with you. I fell in love with you when we first met at that dinner party in London last year, and I moved heaven and earth to get away from Rome and come here when I knew you were to be at Dashbury. Violet, you don't love your husband, you practically admitted it."

Ludovic came closer to her and took her hand. "Come away with me, my darling, and you can get a divorce and we will be married, and then go away to Italy and you can forget all about London and the world, and I'll tell Uncle Hugh that I don't want his money or this great mausoleum of a house and let him do whatever he likes with it."

Violet tried to pull her hand away. She sat straight up. "But Ludovic, I couldn't, I couldn't. I should be disgraced, a divorced woman. I should be cut by all the people who matter and who hate me. Think of the gossip, the fuss, and leaving my child."

"But you don't bother much with him," said Ludovic candidly.

"You can't possibly understand a mother's feelings," said Violet, with stately gentleness.

"You're only making the child an excuse. If you loved me you'd forget about him and be content to see him sometimes. Once for all, do you love me?"

"I . . . I . . ."

He threw his arms round her and kissed her passionately.

The door was flung open, and Hugh walked into the room. His face was blank with amazement. Violet disentangled herself from Ludovic and stood staring at her uncle.

The gilded hands of the clock on the mantelpiece had moved only a fraction but to the three people in the room it seemed like time stolen from eternity. Hugh was the first to speak.

"I came down to my study to find a paper, I heard voices

153

in here and I came in to see . . . this. Ludovic, you will perhaps give me some explanation of your conduct and you of yours, Violet."

Violet dabbed her eyes with her handkerchief. "You're very unkind, Uncle Hugh," she said. "Ludovic lost his head and misunderstood."

"What have you got to say, Ludovic?" said Hugh harshly.

Ludovic stood facing his uncle. "I take the entire blame," he said. "I asked Violet to come and talk to me here. As she said, I lost my head, and I am very sorry."

"I should think so," said Hugh. He looked at the clock. "Violet, you'd better go upstairs and I should like you to leave here tomorrow. And you, Ludovic, come and see me directly after breakfast."

Violet gave a sob and with a swish of her skirts swept across the room, snatching up her candlestick and wrenching open the door. The two men heard the scratch of a match being lighted, and her footsteps echoing across the silent hall.

They stood facing each other. The air of the room grew heavier and more oppressive. Mundell had brought in pots of jonquils and had arranged them in a group in the graceful *jardinière* inherited from the eighteenth century. They threw out their scent in waves and ever afterwards Ludovic felt sickened by their sight and perfume. Hugh was furiously angry but he kept a hold on his temper.

"I don't think there's anything more to be said tonight," he said curtly. "If you can make any explanation of your conduct, I will listen to you tomorrow. Turn out the lamps please."

Three people at Dashbury Park passed a sleepless night. In her fourposter bed Violet tore the edge of her lace-trimmed handkerchief with her teeth. What a fool she had been to go downstairs and meet Ludovic! But her anger with herself soon passed and was replaced by self-pity. Ludovic had behaved outrageously and got beyond her control and Uncle Hugh had been intolerable and had not taken her side and had asked her to leave. How was she to explain the curtailment of her visit to her husband? Luckily he was still away in the north of England. She would send off an early telegram telling the servants to get the house ready and then, well, there were always distractions to be had in London and she could tell Henry when he returned some convincing tale. Her head ached. If only she could prevent any of this getting to her husband's ears! She must try and see Ludovic and impress this on him, but her uncle would of course have to explain her sudden departure to his wife. A clock chimed, and Violet, who had a deep respect for the importance to her looks of beauty sleep, pushed the torn handkerchief under her pillow and resolutely shut her eyes. But sleep was long in coming.

Hugh walked rapidly up to his room, pulled back the curtains of the tall window and looked at the moonlit park. He stared at the familiar scene, his head throbbing with fatigue and anger. The week in London had been exceptionally tiring and difficult. An old friend had come to him in deep distress about money, and Hugh had helped him, though it seemed certain that the position could not be retrieved by what he had been able to give. The city was pessimistic about the political situation, agricultural prices were not stable, and Hugh had come home as he hoped to rest. He had been unable to sleep, and had gone downstairs to fetch a paper to read. After finding it on his table he had come into the hall and walked out of the darkness, a small lamp in his hand. The feeling of darkness and stillness had been soothing; the moon shone through the windows at the top of the hall, touching here a fresco and there the banisters with light, and the pagodas glimmered a little. Suddenly the sound of voices struck on his ear. He stopped dead and listened. There had been a spectacular burglary in a country house ten miles away the winter before this and Hugh took a large walking stick from the rack of sticks and umbrellas by the front door, flung open the drawing-room door, and could scarcely believe what he saw. But it was no moment to think back on events. The necessary thing was to see what to do next morning. He must try and get some sleep, and forget his anger and astonishment.

Ludovic walked up and down his room in an anguish of misery, doubt and unhappiness. In the small hours of the morning he fell on his bed fully dressed and, being young, was able to fall into a fitful sleep.

27

THE following morning Lucy woke with a sense of foreboding. She was disquieted about Ludovic, and Katharine's obvious unhappiness had saddened her. The whole household started the day with their usual feelings of frustration, fatigue or moderate happiness. Sarah felt the weight of her years, Bourton's corns were hurting him, and Mrs. Robson wondered why the great kitchen range was giving such unsatisfactory heat; she sent her head kitchen-maid Maud flying hither and thither, rebuking her for stupidity, while Maud's own mind was on the meaning glance given to her by the gardener's boy James as they emerged from church last Sunday.

To Violet, Ludovic and Hugh the clear freshness of the

day brought no comfort or solace. Violet breakfasted in her room, Ludovic missed family prayers and was so late into the dining-room for breakfast that Louise and Lucy had left before he arrived. Hugh had breakfasted early, embattled behind his newspaper, and had spoken no word to anyone. Louise and Lucy ate in silence. Hugh was in one of his moods, thought Louise, as he left the room.

Violet had sent a note by her maid to Louise to say that she was unfortunately obliged to leave that day and Louise came along to her bedroom. Violet had built up a structure part truth, part fiction. Henry's old aunt had, she said, just come to London unexpectedly and Henry wanted Violet there to take her for drives and entertain her. In fact the aunt had been in London already for some weeks and was going to stay on several more, but Louise accepted this excuse. Hugh had not so far told her about the episode of last night, but Louise suspected part of the truth and was thankful that Violet was leaving. She had become more and more disturbed about Ludovic and dreaded Hugh's disapproval when he returned from London. She had just let things slide. She had meant to speak to Violet and urge her to leave Ludovic alone, and had also meant to warn Ludovic that he should leave Dashbury. She had in fact drifted along from day to day doing nothing.

Hugh was sitting at his writing desk when Ludovic came in. Both men showed the effects of their lack of sleep: Ludovic had cut himself shaving, Hugh had dark patches under his eyes and the lines on his face seemed more deeply engraved.

After a curt "Good morning" he asked Ludovic to sit down. He leant forward and pushed back the silver-mounted inkstand. As his fingers touched the hoof he wished for a moment that he was riding across country on his good horse with the wind in his face.

"You wished to speak to me?" Ludovic's voice was cold and harsh.

"I did. We won't go into what happened last night or your behaving in a certain way. I can only say that if you wish to have an intrigue with a married woman, please do not carry it on in my house, with someone related to you by marriage."

"I don't know what you call an intrigue," said Ludovic furiously. "I admit I was foolish and lost my head, but there was nothing worse."

There was a moment's silence and then Hugh continued as if Ludovic had not spoken: "I am concerned that this should never reach the ears of Violet's husband, and I am prepared to say if you and Violet will give me a solemn promise never to speak of this to anyone whatever, that I myself will never refer to it again. Violet is leaving today. She has told Louise that she is obliged to go back to London and Louise has accepted the excuse. You will leave tomorrow for Rome after promising that you will not make any attempt to see Violet as you pass through London."

Ludovic sat silently staring down at the carpet. He lifted his head. "I must see her again," he said. "She must choose between me and her husband. She could come to Italy with me."

"My dear boy," said Hugh, "are you so mad as to think that Violet would leave her husband, her position in society, and run off abroad with you? You must indeed, I think, be mad. You'd have to leave the Embassy, and when you succeed me can you imagine establishing a divorced woman here even if she was your wife?"

Ludovic leapt to his feet. "But I don't want to succeed, I don't want this great big house, with all its responsibilities and properties. I want to live in my own way, the way I like."

There is a dark place in all of us which we call the back of our minds. It is full of fears which we hesitate to confront. When these fears are dragged out by someone else and thrown at us in raw, crude words, the effect is of delayed action and strikes with an unbearable pain.

Hugh rose to his feet, his face whitening. "Very well, Ludovic," he said, "we won't discuss this. You may think differently some day. But in the meantime if you wish to speak to Violet you can of course do so."

He gave the bell-pull by the mantelpiece a heavy tug. There was a depressing silence in the room. Ludovic could not meet his uncle's look. Hugh seemed to have aged in the last few minutes.

When Bourton came in, Hugh said: "Will you ask Lady Ashendon to come and speak to me in the library?"

When Bourton had left, Hugh said: "Go into the library and talk to her. I shall not be present. And please shut the door after you."

Violet walked slowly downstairs to the library and came in with a look of gentle innocence on her face.

She started when she saw Ludovic. "Uncle Hugh sent for me," she said.

"He wanted me to talk to you. He says that if I don't see you in London, and if you and I give him the promise not to mention what happened last night to anyone, he will never speak of it again. Those are his terms."

Violet drew a long breath of relief.

"He's not thinking of either you or me, he's thinking about your husband," said Ludovic bitterly. "He says that I am to start back to Rome tomorrow, and not see you in London as I pass through. It is unbearable, intolerable."

"Oh, no, Ludovic dear. We mustn't meet again. Uncle Hugh is quite right. Henry must never know."

"Meaning that you don't care for me, that you have led

me on only for your own amusement. I've taken the blame, I don't mind doing that, but you know in your heart of hearts whose fault it is."

The ever-ready tears came into Violet's eyes and she dabbed them with her handkerchief.

"In other words," Ludovic went on, "you won't throw your cap over the windmill for me. You will go on doing this, making man after man fall in love with you to feed your vanity and sense of power, and give nothing in return. I'm through with you. Goodbye." And he rushed from the room, slamming the door with a reverberation which made the pagodas shake their little bells and the chandelier give out a tinkling sound. Violet's tears flowed when she got back to her room, but they were tears of exquisite relief and not of sorrow.

28

JANE DASHBURY did not see Violet again before she left. Lucy was busy upstairs in Ada's room and Ludovic had departed for a long walk, so Louise and Violet sat together in her sitting-room. Louise seemed preoccupied. Ludovic's name was not mentioned between them.

Violet would have given a great deal to know whether her aunt knew of the previous night's episode in the library. She must have noticed Ludovic's infatuation for her— Violet was sure of that, although Louise had made no comment upon it. They talked of the London season and of the balls which were to be given, and then gossiped for a little about mutual acquaintances. Lady X's name somehow came up.

"I don't like her," said Louise. "She's always making nasty insinuations about people and looking very innocent. She does it and everyone knows."

"Yes," said Violet, "people who live in glass houses shouldn't throw stones."

Louise glanced sharply at her but Violet's face was completely blank and expressionless.

"No, they certainly should not," replied Louise.

At that moment Hugh came into the room. He greeted Violet with cold politeness but didn't relax the severity of his expression and asked Louise a curt question about his mother's health.

Bourton announced luncheon, adding that Mr. Ludovic had not yet come in.

"We won't wait for him," said Hugh. When Lucy joined them they filed into the dining-room.

Ludovic did not appear and his name was not mentioned. Hugh talked briefly about his week in London, addressing his remarks to his wife, while Lucy sat in silence and Violet crumbled the roll beside her plate. It was a relief when the meal was over, and Violet went upstairs to put on her hat.

Her departure under the pillars of the porch was to the outward eye a decorous family leavetaking. Louise and she embraced, Hugh gave her a brief handshake, and she waved to Lucy as she mounted the steps into the victoria, and settling herself on the seat gave the group in the porch a dazzling smile. The horses started and the victoria rolled away.

Lucy glanced at Hugh. 'How tired he looks,' she thought. 'I wonder why. I expect he's had a hard time in London.' Her relations with Hugh had never gone beyond kindly formality on his part and a shy avoidance of him on hers, so she said nothing.

Now he looked at her keenly. She suddenly seemed prettier, her hair had a new sparkle and her eyes looked brighter.

He paused before going into his study. "How did Mr. Maxwell get on with the books?" he asked.

"Very well, I think," she replied. "He has taken the list away with him. I have copied it out. Shall I bring it to you?"

"Yes, please do, I should like to see it."

When Lucy brought in the sheets of paper Hugh took them and ran his eyes down the pages in the same way as he would have treated a bank statement, but with less comprehension. He laid them on the table.

"Has he finished the work here?" Hugh asked. "Will he be coming again?"

"He said he would come if you wished it." As she said this she coloured a little. "He has taken away several books which you said he might show to some Oxford scholars. He'll bring them back if you didn't want them at once."

"No, I don't want them at all." A sharp pang assailed him as he remembered Ludovic's words. He heard an echo of the young man's voice, 'But I don't want to succeed. I don't want this great big house and all its responsibilities.'

Hugh clenched his hands and struck the table. He looked up to see Lucy looking timidly at him.

"Thank you, Lucy," he said, "I am grateful for your help."

Thus dismissed, Lucy left him. Hugh sat down to his writing table, his head in his hands. All the work of his life seemed to have gone for nothing. He raised his head. Ludovic must be made to see reason, but reason was not enough. Dashbury Park would only exist if the owner of it worked for it and loved it. No, reason was clearly not enough.

29

LUDOVIC had gone for a cross-country walk, frowning and furious. The exercise had brought some relief to his mind, though he would not have admitted it. He plunged along leafy lanes and made his way through woods. He knew very little of the countryside and had no sense of the direction in which he was going. As he came round a bend in the road he was surprised to find himself on the outskirts of Dashbury. He walked on until he found himself in the market square. The grass in the centre was a tender green and the trees were showing their pale green leaves tossed by a light wind. There was an air of mild bustle and cheerfulness in the passers-by which accorded ill with Ludovic's mood. He turned into the churchyard which with daffodils and primroses looked gay and inviting.

He stopped under the yew tree and stared at Maria Taynton's solitary headstone. Under the spreading branches there was silence and a kind of musty chill. Ludovic stared in front of him.

"Poor Maria," he said, half aloud, "she died a victim of love." He gazed at the tombstone, then slowly his sense of proportion reasserted itself. He moved away smiling a little. He was beginning to feel much hungrier than a rejected lover should feel. He walked across the square and found the innkeeper, who greeted him with interest and pleasure, and set before him some cold beef and cheese and some beer. He stood in the doorway of the inn courtyard answering questions about the family at Dashbury Park. A girl drove in under the archway. She pulled up her pony, handed the reins to the ostler, and, grasping her skirt, descended onto the cobbled pavement of the yard.

She turned and saw Ludovic. They both gave a start of surprise and stared back at each other. Katharine recovered first and she held out her hand and said good morning. Ludovic, conscious of his dusty shoes and rumpled hair, shook hands silently. Katharine remarked that she came on an errand for her father about his horses and Ludovic said he had been out for a long country walk.

The innkeeper regarded them with a benevolent curiosity which irritated Ludovic and embarrassed Katharine.

"Well, I must be going," he said, "I've been, as I say, for a long walk and I missed luncheon at Dashbury."

They said goodbye and Ludovic walked rapidly away, the soreness of his mind added to by annoyance with himself at having been so brusque.

He had read for a moment in Katharine's eyes a soft kindness and a sort of compassion, and Violet's remarks about her came into his mind. He quickened his pace along the dusty road, passed through the large gates, down the hill, came into view of the house and entered the hall which struck cool and silent. He mounted the stairs to his bedroom.

The drawing-room windows were opened on to the terrace.

Ludovic came in to find the family taking their places for tea. He made brief apologies to Louise for missing luncheon, and she accepted them without comment. Lucy looked at him and looked away again. Ada had not yet returned from London and Hugh came in late for tea. It passed as heavily as meals do when every chance remark may tumble the speaker into the depths of awkwardness. After Hugh had returned to his study Ludovic said that he must go upstairs and put some of his books ready to be packed.

Lucy left the room meaning to get her hat to go out into the garden and found Ludovic outside the bedroom which

Violet had occupied, lost in unhappy thought. He started when he saw her. She longed to help him in his unhappiness and then an axiom of her father's came into her mind. If you are unhappy go straight out and help someone who needs it. "I'll try and turn his thoughts," she said to herself, and she came to a sudden decision and said in a low voice: "Ludovic, Mr. Maxwell has asked me to go and spend a day at Oxford and go on the river there and see the colleges."

Ludovic seemed to come back from a long way off. "Mr. Maxwell?" he repeated. "Oh, yes, George." He looked at her. "Well, yes, do go."

"But I don't see how I can. He wants me to stay in London with some friends of his, some Scotch people. He is a barrister."

"Well, why not go?"

"But I know Aunt Ada will try and prevent it. She'll probably find heaps of things for me to do, and," she lowered her voice almost to a whisper, "and I haven't got any money, and I'm rather shabby."

Ludovic stared at her and then a thought struck him. "I'll speak to Uncle Hugh," he said. "If he says you're to go, you'll go."

Lucy looked dubious. "Never mind," said Ludovic, "don't worry. I'll settle it with him. And give my best wishes to George for . . . for everything. I shan't see him or you for some time. I must go and see to my things."

He left her, his mind full of a resolution he had not felt before.

After a dinner which dragged through mostly in silence, when Ludovic and his uncle were left alone over their port, Ludovic said,

"I want to ask you something."

"Go on," said Hugh. His voice was not encouraging.

"George Maxwell has asked Lucy to go to Oxford for a

165

day. There are some friends of his with whom she can stay for a day or two in London. Can she go? And can she go with them to Oxford for the day?"

"She can certainly go as far as I'm concerned. Has she spoken to your aunts about it?"

"No," said Ludovic, "Aunt Ada won't want her to go. She never wants Lucy to go anywhere. And another thing, Lucy hasn't any money for her railway fare."

"Who are these people he wants her to stay with?"

"His name is Alastair McAndrew. He's a lawyer."

Hugh frowned. "I've heard that name somewhere this week. Yes, they were talking about him at the Club. It seems he is a rising man who may go far. They should be suitable people for Lucy to stay with. I will give her some money."

"Thank you, Uncle Hugh, I will tell Lucy when she hears from George, to speak to you."

There was a silence, full with heaviness, while Ludovic screwed up his courage. "Can I come into the library and talk to you for a few minutes?"

"Certainly," said Hugh.

They sat down in two leather armchairs on opposite sides of the fireplace.

"I'm sorry about what I said this morning," said Ludovic, "about not wanting to have this place."

Hugh shifted in the armchair, his hands grasped the arms tightly. "It's just as well," he said, "I've known it for some time. I can't deny that it's a very heavy blow to me. I've worked so hard and so long to keep everything together here. Your father loved this place, and when he died my only thought was to pass it on to you with the estate in as good shape as possible. Since your recent visits here I've seen you consider it all so burdensome, and that you don't seem to have any wish to assume your responsibilities or take up your duties here. Your forebears lived and died here, and I did not think that you would seriously consider turning your back on it and making a life for yourself without duties or responsibilities in Italy. I know that your work is considered good by your chief in Rome and that you could probably join the Diplomatic Service, but may I point out to you that if you were an Englishman living abroad you would not be in a very good position to represent the ideas of your own country."

Ludovic, who had appeared flushed during dinner, had become very white. He had listened in complete silence to his uncle's speech, the longest he had ever heard Hugh make.

"This has been a most disagreeable day, for yourself and for me," Hugh went on more kindly. "You've behaved like a gentleman, taking all the blame for what happened last night on yourself, and I am pleased with you in that respect." He sighed. "With regard to the question of things here, it would be better to leave it alone for the moment. After what has happened in the last fortnight I can well understand that you can't feel anything but bitterness and unhappiness here."

He rose. "And now, go to bed. You've a long journey before you."

30

LUDOVIC took Lucy aside before his early start the following morning and told her of his talk with Hugh. "When you hear from George go straight and tell Uncle Hugh. There won't be any difficulty."

Lucy thanked him. She dared not sympathise with him openly about Violet, but in her face she showed her distress.

He said awkwardly, "Don't worry about me. I shall be all right." He put a little leather bag into her hand saying in a hurried voice, "Get yourself something; a nice gown or something when you are in London," and before she could look at it and thank him he was gone through the hall door. Lucy fled upstairs to her room and opened the little bag. It contained a collection of sovereigns and half sovereigns. She burst into tears.

"Ludovic is kind and generous. He's good. Oh! I hope he never sees Violet again!"

Hugh visited his mother and they talked for a little.

"I suppose you realise what has happened to Ludovic," Hugh said.

"I felt much disturbed," she replied, "and very unhappy. Ludovic came in to see me but he looked so haggard and worn, poor boy."

"Louise should have stopped it," said Hugh.

"No, I don't imagine she could, Hugh. She might perhaps have spoken to Violet, but from what I know of her it wouldn't have stopped her. She could have said that she couldn't help it if men fell in love with her."

"Well, it might have checked her a bit."

"Don't be hard on Louise, Hugh. It was difficult for her to speak to her own niece in this house about your nephew."

Hugh frowned irritably. "Well, I hope not much mischief's done. I suppose the servants are all chattering about it."

"I fear so; I've had to shut Soey up about it several times, but luckily they don't know that you found the two together last night in the drawing-room. But of course they speculate about Violet's and Ludovic's sudden departures."

168

"I don't mind as long as nothing reaches Henry's ears. What about Theresa? I hear that she and her stepdaughter came to tea. I gather from Louise that Violet behaved discreetly and went into the garden with Katharine and Lucy afterwards. Well, we must hope it's all right."

"Indeed, I hope as you do, my dear Hugh, that nothing will reach Henry's ears, but I am not only concerned about him. I'm concerned about Ludovic. For a young man to fall in love with someone like Violet leads to cynicism and a bitterness which is hard to get over. It leaves its mark."

Hugh sat silent as she continued: "I'm very fond of Ludovic. Before I die I should like to see him in a fair way to being happy."

"You're not going to die yet, Mother, and Ludovic's young. He'll recover."

Jane made no answer to this piece of optimism.

"Nothing need be said to Ada," said Hugh as he left the room. "She's been away most of the time and Louise won't speak of it to anyone."

Jane closed her eyes and her mind was troubled.

When Ada returned, she brought with her some large, heavy cardboard boxes which had to be brought up the back stairs after they'd been removed from the luggage cart.

Ada had an air of triumphant busyness as she entered the house. After Violet's departure, and then Ludovic's, the house had settled back into a sort of quiet. Lucy had had time to take a volume out and sit in the temple in the Pleasure Ground, where thoughts both painful and pleasant assailed her. The whole episode of Violet and Ludovic had deeply troubled her, while her own happiness at George's invitation, and Ludovic's putting aside his own trouble in helping her, had moved her to tears. She had looked at the leather bag and counted the money. It seemed to her like a fortune. 'I shall always keep the little leather bag,' she thought, 'when I have spent the money,' and she mentally reviewed her wardrobe.

The upper servants had a great deal to talk about and the under ones gossiped behind their backs. Violet's maid had been tiresomely discreet. She knew that if any chatter about her mistress reached Violet's ears she would be faced with instant dismissal. She had merely looked mysterious and had shaken her head slightly. Nothing more.

For four days after Ada's return no letter came from George Maxwell, and Lucy, who had run down early each morning to look on the marble table between the pagodas, found no envelopes addressed to her. She turned away with a sharp stab of disappointment.

Jane saw her altered looks with misgiving. Lucy had perhaps misunderstood George. No, that wasn't possible. George Maxwell, she knew, was a man of few words, but when he spoke those words they were deliberate and his ideas were clear and definite. Then the thought crossed her mind that Ada had come in early to see her. She said she was obliged to go into Dashbury to consult with the clergyman on the subject of the bazaar to be held in the town. Jane recalled that there was something a little hurried and furtive about her manner. She closed her eyes and thought. She would have given all her possessions to be active and able to walk about. It would be so easy now to sink back and let everything slide and just lie there, taking pain and little bits of pleasure as they came. But no, she could still help. She lay there in silence and rang the handbell for Soey, who came in immediately.

Jane said: "Will you go to Miss Ada's room and look on her writing table for my little seal which she borrowed? The one with the Dashbury arms on it. And, oh yes, will you look and see if there's a letter addressed to me amongst Miss Ada's papers? I have an idea she may have picked up a lot of letters in a hurry this morning, and there may be one for me or one of the other members of the family," Jane ended.

Soey's lips tightened. "Very well, m'lady."

She returned about half an hour later. She handed the little seal to her mistress, and a letter. It was addressed to Lucy and had the device of an Oxford college on the back flap of the envelope.

"I couldn't find the letter addressed to you, m'lady, but here is the one for Miss Lucy."

Jane thanked her, merely remarking that the letter from her cousin, Lady Mary, must have been delayed by her ill-health. Soey said nothing, but looked as if she would have liked to say a very great deal.

"Will you ask Miss Lucy to come and see me?" said Jane, and Soey departed with alacrity on this errand. When Lucy came, a little breathless, Jane said:

"This is for you, Lucy. I asked Soey to go and find me a seal I had lent to Ada. In looking for it she found this letter to you. Ada must have caught up some letters by mistake in the hall before she went out."

Their eyes met for a fraction of a second. "Sit down here and read the letter if you like."

George's letter was not long, but it enclosed an invitation from Mrs. McAndrew to stay for two nights in London and to spend the intervening day at Oxford. His own letter said:

"Dear Miss Lucy,—It would give my friends Mr. and Mrs. Alastair McAndrew great pleasure if you will come and stay for two nights with them in London, from Monday to Wednesday, and travel down to Oxford with Mrs. McAndrew on the Tuesday, when I will show you the sights. I hope you will find it possible to do this and that you will write to Mrs. McAndrew and accept her invitation.

And then she will meet you when you reach London at the station. If you do this I shall look forward to a very pleasant time.

"Yours very sincerely,
GEORGE MAXWELL."

Lucy's face lit up with a sober pleasure. She handed the letter to Jane. Jane read it and then looked at the date. It was dated three days before. She gave a small exclamation.

"Is anything wrong, Cousin Jane?" Lucy's voice was anxious.

"Nothing with the letter, my child. It's been delayed."

"So it has," said Lucy. "I'd expected it sooner. I had wondered. I mean, I had thought he must have changed his mind."

Jane looked at Lucy. "As I told you, I sent Soey along to Ada's room to find a little seal I'd lent her and see if any letters of mine had got mixed up with hers. Soey found this and brought it to me. Ada must have picked it up by mistake."

"I see," said Lucy.

"Well, never mind now, but see Louise. Hugh will have told her that you are to go to London and Oxford. And write to Mrs. McAndrew and Mr. Maxwell and bring the letters here to me."

"But Aunt Ada has given me some envelopes to address, ever so many."

"Never mind. I will explain to her why you haven't done them. Go at once, my dear, to Louise and, yes, I think it would be best if you brought the letters here to write."

In her bodily and mental pain, Jane was bracing herself to the effort of speaking to Ada.

Lucy returned quickly, her cheeks pink. "Aunt Louise has been so kind. She said she is going to give me a reticule

and a petticoat, and that Uncle Hugh will give me the money
to go to London."

"I shall give you something to spend, too."

Lucy told her about Ludovic's present.

"Ludovic's got a good heart," said his grandmother.
"I'm glad he did this for you just at that moment."

"Do you think he will get over Violet; I mean . . .?"

"In time," said Jane. "But as I said to Hugh, a love affair
with a married woman like Violet on the threshold of a young
man's life is apt to bring a cynical outlook. Poor Ludovic.
And now write your letters, my dear."

Lucy did so, finding them both difficult. She tried to
imagine what the unknown McAndrews would look like and
how they would behave. After several false starts she wrote
to George and then to Mrs. McAndrew and brought Jane
the letters to read.

"Very nice, my dear," said Jane. "You write a good
clear hand and express yourself nicely."

When Lucy had left her, Jane tried to read for a little, but
her thoughts were elsewhere. She shut the book and Ada
came in with her hat on.

"I've just come to see you, Mother. I've had a very satisfactory talk with Mr. Brown and he and his wife agreed
with all my suggestions about the bazaar. But I can't
trust her not to rearrange everything when my back is
turned."

"Well, after all, it's the parish bazaar, my dear, and
people are apt to want to do things in their own way."

"I can't allow that," said Ada, "and in my opinion it
should be properly done."

"I want to speak to you, Ada. I sent Soey to look in
your writing table for the little seal I lent you and I told
her to see if there were any . . . if by any chance you had
gathered up one or two . . . of my letters in a hurry. I've

had no letter from Mary." Jane paused. Ada's lips had tightened. "She didn't find my letter but she found one for Lucy from Mr. Maxwell at Oxford and brought it to me."

Ada flushed a dark red. "Yes, I must have picked it up with mine," she said.

"Lucy showed it to me," went on her mother, "and it is dated three days ago."

There was a deathly silence in the room.

"However," continued Jane, "I hope there is no harm done. Mr. Maxwell has invited Lucy to go to Oxford for a day and friends of his have invited her to stay with them in London."

"Surely it is most unsuitable for Lucy to go and stay with people we know nothing about."

"Hugh knows about the husband, Mr. McAndrew. He wishes Lucy to go and is paying for her journey."

Ada rubbed her hands together. She looked down at her grey skirt.

"Do you and Hugh want to throw Lucy into the arms of an Oxford professor?"

Jane replied patiently: "It's not a question of throwing Lucy into anyone's arms, Ada. Lucy has had so little pleasure in life, she should not be denied this one."

"Just at this moment," burst out Ada, "when I've brought back all the pamphlets and invitations to be sent out for the big meeting in London! I'd counted on Lucy's help. They're very short-handed in their London office and I offered to bring back the pamphlets to be sent out from here."

"Well, if there is no urgent hurry, Lucy can help you when she gets back. My dear Ada, don't spoil things for the child, she's had much unhappiness and is an orphan."

"She's been very lucky to come here, to be housed and fed and allowed to do useful work."

174

"Being housed and fed and being given useful work is not the be-all and end-all of existence," said Jane. "And now, my dear, you will want to take off your hat, and I must rest for a little."

31

Hugh summoned Lucy to his room and gave her the money for the fare to London and Oxford.

She stammered her thanks.

"Not at all, you deserve it," he said. "Enjoy yourself, and give my regards to Mr. Maxwell. I hope he will return here and I shall be glad to welcome him." He looked at Lucy as if he were seeing her for the first time. Her face was becomingly flushed and her eyes bright.

When she had left the room he sat down with the feeling of satisfaction of one who has done a good deed, and waited for a moment before he plunged into the papers on his writing table. It might have been nice to have a daughter, he thought with a sigh.

Ada had grimly pointed to the large cardboard boxes stacked in the corners of her room, and Lucy settled down to the work of looking out addresses in books and addressing envelopes. She only paused from the busy scratching of her own pen to gaze out of the window at the scene outside.

Louise roused herself to take an interest in Lucy's clothes, and even proposed to give her a dress of her own, for use in the evening when Lucy was staying with the McAndrews.

Lucy was summoned to Louise's bedroom where several dresses were laid out on the bed. One of those was to be fitted on Lucy, who had a slighter figure, by Louise's maid, and Louise in a sudden excess of generosity presented Lucy with a small seed pearl necklace.

Ada frowned and fumed when Lucy was taken away to fit on the dress. Louise, with secret pleasure, spun out the fittings for as long as possible, and Lucy was obliged to run panting from one to the other.

She had received another letter from George saying how glad he was that she could come to Oxford, also that he was communicating with Mrs. McAndrew on the subject of trains to Oxford.

Mrs. McAndrew also wrote, and though her note was expressed in formal terms kindness shone through the lines written in her fine, tidy script. She said she would meet Lucy at the London terminus.

"A very nice, ladylike sort of letter," was Jane's comment when Lucy showed it to her.

What with addressing envelopes and all the other duties which she had to perform and the careful packing of her small possessions, the days flew by and the morning arrived when Lucy had to leave.

The evening before she left Jane had given her an envelope containing a five-pound note.

"To add to what Ludovic gave you," she said with a smile.

"Oh, Cousin Jane, but you mustn't."

"Don't rob me of my pleasure in giving it to you, my dear. It makes me happy to do it."

Lucy stood the following morning in the porch, clinging to an umbrella and a bag. Hugh came out of the front door and when Lucy drove away she smiled a little. 'I wish she smiled more often,' he thought.

The journey to London was uneventful for most of the passengers in the train, but to Lucy it was fraught with interest. When she arrived at the London terminus she stepped out of the train and stood for a moment bewildered by the clouds of steam which made the atmosphere heavy. She grasped her modest bag, and at that moment felt a touch on her shoulder and turned and found a lady standing there.

"I'm Elspeth McAndrew and you must be Miss Lucy Taynton. The porter will take your bag. Welcome to London."

Mrs. McAndrew was quietly dressed. Her eyes were brown and lively, her hair was auburn and her cheeks had the bright colouring which went with it.

The small brougham went along slowly, avoiding the larger and statelier carriages and large brewers' drays.

"My husband will not be home until this evening, so we can have our luncheon and go anywhere you like to see the sights this afternoon."

Lucy summoned up her courage. "Could I go to a shop? I haven't a dress to wear tomorrow."

Mrs. McAndrew gave her a shrewd glance and marked the shabbiness of Lucy's clothes, also her neatness, and the perfection of several darns visible on her gloves.

"Certainly," she replied. "I take it that you will not be wanting to go to a very expensive place. They can charge awful high prices in London."

"No," said Lucy, colouring to the roots of her hair. "I don't want to buy anything very expensive."

"I will take you first to a little dressmaker woman and we'll see if she can help."

The brougham stopped at a small house in a square which to a more worldly eye than Lucy's would have seemed quiet and unfashionable. Lucy's bag was collected by a neat maid and she entered a pleasant hall from which the staircase mounted covered with plain red carpet.

Luncheon was expeditiously served by the little maid and Elspeth McAndrew talked to Lucy about her life in Edinburgh, how she and Mr. McAndrew had been in London only for two years.

"It's a dirty, smoky place compared with Edinburgh," she said, "and I miss my friends. But my husband is happy here."

The visit to the dressmaker proved a great success. She lived in a little shop at the back of which two apprentices worked. She welcomed Mrs. McAndrew with pleasure and on being told what her errand was she begged the two ladies to be seated.

When Mrs. McAndrew explained that Lucy would need the dress to wear tomorrow, Madame Vera's face clouded for a moment but then became wreathed in smiles. She ran to the cupboard and produced a dress, explaining that it had been returned to her as the young lady for whom it had been made had suddenly had to go into mourning.

"It would fit the young lady well," she said.

"But it's blue," faltered Lucy, "and I'm still in mourning."

"How long ago did your father die?" asked Mrs. McAndrew.

"Nearly two years ago."

"Well, you can't go on mourning for ever," said Mrs. McAndrew. "Try it on, it's not as if it were a bright blue, in fact you might call it a grey-blue."

Lucy allowed herself to be persuaded and the dress fitted her nearly perfectly. She threw a look of agonised shyness at Mrs. McAndrew, who nodded her head comprehendingly.

"You'll be wanting to know the price before you go any farther."

Madame paused, and with a great air of calculation, named the sum upon which she had long since decided in her own mind.

It was well within Lucy's means and she opened her bag to find the money while Madame explained to Mrs. McAndrew that she was only letting it go at this price because it had been returned.

Mrs. McAndrew turned away and looked out of the window at the dingy little street outside, while Lucy counted out the sovereigns. As they went away with the dress neatly packed in swathes of paper in a box, Mrs. McAndrew asked, "Will you not be needing some gloves and shoes?"

Lucy admitted the necessity of these.

That evening Mr. McAndrew returned remarking, "How are you, dearest?" to his wife, and shaking hands with Lucy. He looked at her smiling. His forehead was square and his mouth a tight line, but his eyes looked friendly and amused.

Dinner was soon over. Lucy thought of the long-drawn-out elaboration of the meals at Dashbury, and enjoyed eating plain food quickly. During dinner her host told them of his day's work and Mrs. McAndrew related what they had done.

He darted an amused look at Lucy. "A dress to wear tomorrow? It is new to me that Oxford should be considered a dressy place. Surely they live for study and higher thoughts there?"

"Don't tease Miss Lucy," said his wife, "she has been in mourning and has no chance of getting new dresses in the country. In fine weather like this an old dress shows up very badly and black shows every mark too."

After dinner Mr. McAndrew said he must work on a brief.

Mrs. McAndrew sighed. "A lawyer husband is a terrible thing to have; the better they are doing the harder they have to work, and I am glad of your company."

She opened the piano and sang some Scotch airs in a small but true soprano voice while Lucy, her hands for once idle, listened to the music and her own thoughts.

Tea was brought in, and Mr. McAndrew made his appearance, tired but smiling, and remarking that he hoped the weather would be fine tomorrow.

In her small bedroom Lucy lay awake, thinking how pleasant life was as lived in this quiet little house. Her thoughts reverted to Ludovic. Was it perhaps not so surprising that he wanted a life without heavy responsibilities. She looked back at Dashbury Park and thought of the machinery of hard work and constant care needed to keep it going. The house, the gardens, the stables, the farms, the parkland, the Pleasure Ground. The men and women on the estate to be looked after, then the property in the town of Dashbury. To fit your shoulders into that heavy yoke must be to someone of Ludovic's temperament a hardship which she had never clearly understood before—she fell asleep, meaning to wake early to see what the weather was like.

But she was tired and woke with the sun high in the heavens. A light mist was dispersing and there was the promise of a lovely day.

32

As the train approached Oxford Lucy looked at her companion sitting opposite to her. Mrs. McAndrew's neatly gloved hands were folded in her lap: she was gazing at the passing woods and fields with the utmost composure. 'How nice it must be to be married and so happy,' thought Lucy. Her own mind was in a turmoil of emotion and she was bracing herself with the thought that something might go wrong and the day be a dismal failure; also that she might prove inadequate and stupid.

The train slowed down and the towers of Oxford came into sight, grey amongst the green of the trees and meadows. In a minute more it had stopped, and Lucy saw George through the carriage window. Mrs. McAndrew alighted and Lucy followed her.

George shook hands, looking austere but pleased as he wrung their hands in his strong grip.

The sharp Midland air compounded of the scent of river and water meadows fanned their cheeks.

They stepped out and into an ancient cab whose horse gallantly started down the steepish hill. George sat opposite the two ladies and silence (if silence it could be called with the rattling of the cab over the stones on the hill) would have fallen if Mrs. McAndrew had not smilingly given George an account of her husband's doings. Lucy listened spellbound, her eyes downcast. Then she looked out of the window and then back at George, who smiled gravely at her.

"It is such a beautiful day," he said, "that instead of giving you luncheon in my rooms I have ordered a boat and a picnic—and we will tie up under the bank and eat there. I trust it will not spoil your dresses, but ladies in Oxford seem to like going in boats."

'I wonder,' thought Lucy with a sharp pang, 'if there is any one young lady he takes out in a boat.'

"It won't do our dresses an atom of harm if we are careful," said Mrs. McAndrew briskly, "and if you will hand us in and out of the boat. I have lent Miss Taynton a parasol so that she will get no ill effects from the sun."

Lucy thought she had never seen anything more beautiful than the quadrangle of George's college, with a may tree rosy pink against a grey wall.

He led the way up a steep dark staircase and flung the door open into his room. Even on a brilliant day in early May the room was dark with a panelling which had survived through the years, although each successive year added its quota of smoke and dust. But the room had a neat proportion about it. Above the old mantelpiece was the portrait of a man with a high stock collar. Under a broad brow his eyes looked out with benevolent intelligence. The tables in the room were stacked with leather-bound books, and the scent of tobacco permeated the room.

"There is a good view of the quad from the window," George said, and Mrs. McAndrew and Lucy looked out.

Mrs. McAndrew turned to speak to George and Lucy went on looking out on to the soft square of grass, the red may tree and the grey walls.

Then Mrs. McAndrew recalled Lucy into the room. "George would like to show us some of his books."

The ladies sat down in two well-worn leather chairs, one each side of the fireplace. Mrs. McAndrew, though obviously not bookish, took a lively and sensible interest in everything she was shown, and Lucy listened all eyes and attention. They then visited the Chapel, then slowly strolled through college gardens and made their way to the river.

Lucy's life had been barren of much enchantment and the softly running green water dappled by sunshine, the heady scent of the may, the slow progress of the boat, the feeling of being in a beautiful unknown world where the only sound was distant bells and chiming clocks flushed her face and made her eyes shine.

Mrs. McAndrew had announced that she would steer the

boat; she liked doing it, she said. George rowed with long slow strokes and Lucy sat opposite him.

'She looks pretty, that dress is just right for boating,' thought Mrs. McAndrew. 'I wonder?'

George looked at Lucy. He could not have told whether she had on a new gown or an old one, but as he sat opposite to her he was conscious of a new Lucy, a Lucy who fitted into his world, who was herself no longer only a member of a family in a background unfamiliar to himself. They talked quietly.

He tied the boat under an overhanging tree and the picnic basket was opened. Lucy ate very little, while Mrs. McAndrew being hungry did justice to the food.

After they had finished George asked the ladies' permission to light his pipe. Mrs. McAndrew rose briskly to her feet.

"I am going into that field there," she said. "I see some cowslips. I shall pick them to take back to London."

"Shall I come?" said Lucy.

"Certainly not, you must not desert our host. I shan't be long. Give me a hand, George," and grasping her skirts firmly in one hand she took hold of a branch, walked up a sloping bit of bank and was seen bending over the small yellow flowers grouped all over the field.

George knocked the ashes out of his pipe into the river and put it with deliberate care into his pocket.

"Miss Lucy," he said, "I want to ask you, do you like what you have seen of Oxford?"

"I think it is the most beautiful place I have ever seen."

"It is not always like this," said George, "it can rain very heavily here and the mists rise from the river."

"It rains a lot at Dashbury and we have foggy weather there sometimes," said Lucy smiling.

183

"Then could you be happy here in Oxford with me?"

Lucy's eyes opened widely.

"I mean I am asking you to marry me. I love you. Could you love me?"

Lucy nodded speechlessly.

He leant forward and took her small trembling hands in his own. "Mind you," he said, "I am a poor man; my salary is not large, though I have a little of my own and some day shall have my home in Scotland and a few acres; but we should have enough to live quietly in a small house, Lucy."

The next few minutes went by in the talk of two shy people who can at last speak their minds to each other, as perfume drifted from the fields and the water lapped softly against the sides of the boat. They were existing in an oasis of time just for themselves only with cares and difficulties vanished and forgotten.

Suddenly there was a shriek and a noisy sound of bellowing and Mrs. McAndrew appeared on the edge of the bank flushed and exclaiming: "The bull, he's after me, help me down quick!" George and Lucy sprang to their feet and grasped her arms. Her hands were still tightly clasping a bunch of flowers. She collapsed into the boat on the seat beside Lucy.

"I was gathering flowers in the field, and suddenly through a gap in the hedge rushed this ferocious animal, who came running towards me. Oh, what an escape."

She fanned herself with her handkerchief and wiped her eyes. Lucy put her arms round her and her eyes met George's. He was laughing.

"It's nothing to laugh at, George," said Mrs. McAndrew. The bright colour had returned to her cheeks. "Give me some paper out of the picnic basket and a piece of string. I want to take these flowers back to London. I love flowers and they are an awful price there." Neatly and methodically

184

she rolled the flowers up in paper and Lucy handed her a piece of string.

"A longer piece, please," said Mrs. McAndrew, then she glanced at Lucy's face and then at George's.

"I have just asked Lucy to marry me," he said, "and she has consented, that's why we didn't hear the bull trampling, or indeed anything else."

Mrs. McAndrew laid the flowers carefully on the seat beside her, and gave Lucy a hug and extended a hand to George.

"Alastair will be glad," she said. "He feared you would become one of those old crusted, absent-minded bachelor dons who wander about Oxford."

"Well, I must say," said George, "Alastair kept his opinions about that to himself. He never spoke of this to me."

"Alastair keeps his own counsel," said Elspeth McAndrew. "He knew it was no good speaking until you had found the right person, and last night he said to me about Lucy, 'That's a real nice lassie, she would suit George fine.'"

She rose, walked carefully to the stern of the boat and resumed her steering, while George and Lucy sat opposite to each other smiling.

When they reached the station George said, "I shall write this evening to Lord Dashbury and ask for his consent. Maybe I can come and stay and we could make arrangements."

He pressed Lucy's hand in farewell and waved his hat while the train pulled out of the station.

Lucy and Elspeth were in a carriage alone, the flowers carefully laid on the seat.

"You're a lucky girl," said Elspeth, "Alastair thinks the world of George," and she added, "I would say he is lucky too, my dear. And now I'm going to shut my eyes; that adventure with the bull was very fatiguing."

She slept, and Lucy in a daze of happiness gazed out of the window with unseeing eyes.

As they reached the outskirts of London Mrs. McAndrew woke and straightened her headgear.

"Could I," said Lucy, "have one cowslip to keep? I will press it in my prayer book."

"Certainly, more than one," said Elspeth.

When Lucy came down to dinner, Alastair McAndrew took her hand in his strong grasp.

"Many congratulations, Lucy, you've got a good man and a clever one too. I'm certain you will be happy, as far as we can be certain of anything in this world. You must come again to stay." Then he laughed.

"Elspeth's the heroine," he said. "She's no country girl and she's mortally feared of cows and to venture into a field and be chased by a bull—well!"

33

LOUISE and Ada were having tea when Lucy returned. Louise made some enquiries about her journey and the day at Oxford, but they were so perfunctory that Lucy had no difficulty in answering them.

"Well, Lucy," said Ada, "I hope that now you have had a holiday you will settle down to do some work."

Lucy gave a murmured assent to this and escaped upstairs as soon as she could. She went in to see Jane, who with one glance at her face held out her arms to her.

After a while Jane said, "Have you told Hugh and Louise and Ada?"

"No, I haven't told anybody; but Mr. Maxwell—George—is going to write to Uncle Hugh."

"Then say nothing till he does."

The following morning Hugh came in late to breakfast. He was as usual indisposed for conversation.

Ada rose briskly to her feet when breakfast was finished. "Come Lucy, we must get to work."

Hugh raised his head. "I want to see Lucy," he said.

Lucy's heart gave a bound as they left the room, Ada staring after them.

"Sit down, Lucy," said Hugh. "I have had a letter from Mr. Maxwell, who says that he has asked you to marry him and that you have consented. Is this true?"

"Yes," said Lucy.

"You think you will be happy living in Oxford?"

"Yes," said Lucy again.

"Mr. Maxwell writes with good sense and good feeling," said Hugh. "He tells me his exact financial position and I gather from what he says that you will be able to manage if you live quietly. I hope to settle some small sum on you."

"Oh, Uncle Hugh," Lucy faltered, "you are very kind."

"It is not fitting that a Taynton should go from this house completely penniless," said Hugh. "By the way, he says that if I think it suitable and you agree, you should be married at the start of the Long Vacation in July so that you can go on your wedding journey, and take a little time over it. Scotch people like to get everything cut and dried and settled," he added with a smile. "Well, my dear Lucy, my best wishes for your happiness," he put out his hand and shook hers, "and now go and tell Louise about it."

Her mind in a confusion which left her trembling and a little faint, Lucy sat down in the hall on a red leather-covered chair and clung with her hands to the gold claws on each arm.

The sunlight sifted golden and shining through the windows in long shafts where the dust of years danced in soft grey particles. The gods and goddesses on the walls smiled down on Lucy and the pagodas, symmetrical and remote, stood motionless, striking an exotic note in the fantasy around them. The hall seemed to say to her how much it had seen, what strange things it had harboured, and what dramas had been enacted there.

She woke to reality with a start. Her name was being called: it was Ada's voice. She ran across the hall into the long drawing-room and out onto the terrace, where she saw Louise sitting stitching at a piece of embroidery. It was the first time Lucy had ever ignored a call from Ada.

Louise lifted her head, and looked a little listlessly at her. "What is it?" she said.

"Aunt Louise," said Lucy, pressing her hands together, "Uncle Hugh has told me to come and see you. I, we, he has heard from Mr. Maxwell: he wants to marry me, and Uncle Hugh has given his consent."

"My dear Lucy," said Louise, "are you happy? When did this all happen?"

"He asked me to marry him at Oxford on the river."

Louise enveloped Lucy in an embrace. "Do you love him?"

"Yes," said Lucy, "with all my heart."

"Sit down," said Louise, "and tell me all about it."

Half an hour later Ada came through the french windows. "What *are* you doing, Lucy?"

Louise's eyes narrowed and sparkled a little with malice. "Congratulate Lucy, my dear Ada," she said, "she is going to be married to Mr. Maxwell."

Ada stood as if turned to stone.

Lucy could not get up from her chair, as her knees were trembling.

"May I ask what all this is about?" said Ada.

"Mr. Maxwell proposed to Lucy the day she went to Oxford," said Louise. "She accepted him and they are going to be married."

Ada stared at Louise, and then shifted her glance to Lucy.

"And," continued Louise blandly, "Mr. Maxwell has written to Hugh asking for his consent to the marriage, and Hugh is writing to give it."

There was a long moment of silence.

"I see," said Ada. "Well, Lucy, I only hope you will be happy," and with that she turned her back on them both and marched into the house.

Louise's delicate eyebrows rose and she permitted herself to smile. "Ada doesn't like losing you, my dear; you are far too useful to her. But don't worry too much about it. Hugh is your guardian and as he has given his consent there is nothing more to be said."

But she knew, and Lucy knew, that a great deal more could be said.

Lucy wrote two letters, one to George Maxwell and one to Ludovic. The one to Ludovic told him about her visit to Oxford, that George had asked her to marry him on a river picnic, that she had accepted, that Uncle Hugh had given his consent and that Aunt Louise had been so kind. "Aunt Ada isn't pleased and has sent me to Coventry. She doesn't speak to me at all or even thank me when I go and address envelopes for her. Nothing can spoil my happiness; but I wish she wouldn't, it makes me so uncomfortable and I feel that I am behaving meanly in deserting her".

A letter quickly came back from Ludovic in Rome:

"I had hoped that this would happen from the moment I first saw you together. I am certain that you are right for each other; George makes up his mind slowly but once made up it is for good. I shall try and get over for your wedding. Rome is very crowded and dusty, there are far too many entertainments for my taste, and there is no one here of any interest. George is, by the way (in case you didn't know it), very clever and should get high up in the University world.

"Think of me sometimes. All my congratulations.

"Your affectionate cousin,

LUDOVIC."

34

"WHAT on earth is the matter with Ada?" Hugh was talking to Louise in her sitting-room two days after Lucy had told him of her engagement. "She never speaks at meals and if one asks her anything she's extremely grumpy."

"She's very angry with Lucy for getting engaged."

"Oh, that's it, is it?"

"She is always giving Lucy things to do, and sometimes she works up in Ada's room for hours, and then she runs messages for her to the village and goes into Dashbury. Ada will miss her very much."

"Well, Ada must do her own jobs in future, and by the way, what about you?" asked Hugh.

"Well, I shall miss her too—Mundell has taken quite a fancy to her, and I've had many more flowers for the house since she came than ever before. She gets on well with the servants and even smooths down Mrs. Robson when she is in one of her tempers. But I might get Rhoda to come on a visit; she can help me with parties and my gowns: she is good at that, though I don't think she will do anything for Ada; she doesn't know anything about charitable work, and she and Ada don't like each other anyhow, and she won't run errands in the way Lucy does. Well, I am glad Lucy is going to be married and I hope she will be happy."

"Yes, I hope so too. I like Maxwell; we don't live in the same world, but I can always talk to him: he is a clever, straightforward sort of man."

Hugh prepared to leave the room and Louise said, "Yes, I hope Lucy will be happy, there's not much happiness about nowadays."

Hugh had closed the door while she spoke and walked across the hall to his room. He had not paid much heed to what Louise had been saying. But vividly, almost as if she were in the room, the words came back into his mind, "there's not much happiness about nowadays." He made an impatient movement. Could she have meant more than she seemed to mean? Was she unhappy? No, that wasn't possible: she had everything a woman could want except children, and she had never seemed to mind much about them, or to care much for any of the family children who came to stay at Dashbury.

He took up his vellum-bound bank book and laid it down again with a frown. Certainly his wife had been a little distrait the last few months. He had also noticed, but had scarcely remarked upon the fact, that she was becoming more devout and attending early Communion Service fasting. Hugh's own practice was to attend an occasional Mattins in either Belling or Dashbury Church, and to take Holy Communion on the feast days of the Church. He had hoped that Louise's churchgoing was giving her satisfaction but had not given the matter any consecutive thought so far.

He took up his bank book and became immersed again in figures, which somehow appeared for once lacking in interest.

If Lucy had been less armour-plated with happiness, her days would have been extremely difficult to get through. Ada had congratulated her upon her engagement with such formal politeness that she might have been speaking to a complete stranger.

"I am afraid you will miss the comforts of Dashbury very much, my dear Lucy. I understand that you will have to live very simply in Oxford in a very small house."

"But it will be my own house, Aunt Ada. Of course I shall miss Dashbury, but Aunt Louise says we may visit her every year. Can I help with the envelopes, please?"

"Certainly you can. I don't know how I am to get them done." But Ada felt that the Lucy who settled down so patiently to her tedious task had somehow eluded her for good.

Violet's name was not spoken, and Hugh and Louise devoutly hoped that the incident at Dashbury would be for ever veiled in silence. Ludovic wrote a letter to Hugh, sending him messages from the Ambassador. There was something in the tone of the letter, a kind of friendliness and respect that pleased Hugh. But he had made up his mind not to look into the future. Ludovic's outburst about Dashbury had hurt him so deeply that thinking back over it was like touching a deep-seated wound. Hugh had trained himself in his business relations not to let his mind go on labouring over difficulties. He resolutely banished his conversation with Ludovic to the back of his mind.

Katharine also wrote to Lucy rejoicing in her happiness and saying little of herself except that she was dreading the festivities of the London season, and that her days passed in a rather noisy turmoil of preparations.

George came for a brief visit to Dashbury and Katharine came over without her stepmother one afternoon.

Louise laid herself out to be pleasant and welcoming to George, and Hugh conversed with him with increasing ease. Ada remained aloof, treating George with the barest civility, if indeed it could be called civility. She could not pretend to be deaf when he addressed her in his clear incisive voice, but she answered in monosyllables and appeared to misunderstand the drift of his remarks. He soon left her to her own self-imposed silence. She glanced without comment at the modest garnet ring of entwined hearts which Lucy now wore on her left hand, and left the room abruptly after meals to get on with her work.

"I haven't done anything for Aunt Ada these days," said Lucy remorsefully to Jane Dashbury.

"No, just leave Ada alone, my dear, while your young man is here. You are only engaged once in your life: let it be as happy a time as possible."

So Lucy, absolved, wandered in the park and garden and Pleasure Ground with George. Both shy and naturally silent people, they found endless things to talk about to their happy astonishment; sometimes they sat in the Pleasure Ground hand in hand while the quiet all around them, the occasional fall of a leaf or twig into the pond at their feet, made speech superfluous.

The wedding was to be in early July and Lucy's small trousseau was made by the dressmaker in Dashbury, but Louise presented her with her wedding gown and she again visited Madame Vera, whose small eyes gleamed as she produced patterns to be taken and shown to Louise.

"You don't look like the same young lady. You would set off an ivory white now you've got more colour."

"I was very happy on the day I wore the dress I bought from you," said Lucy smiling.

Katharine and George met, and although they did not seem to have much to say to each other Lucy felt that there was a quick sympathy between them.

Katharine looked at Lucy's clothes and took a gold locket out of her bag. "It belonged to my mother, I want you to have it," she said, while Lucy exclaimed, "I shall wear it on my wedding day."

"I like your friend Katharine," said George when they were next alone. "She's got that sense which is called commonsense and is rarer than people suppose. She would suit Ludovic very well."

"But——"

"Yes, I saw what was happening. He lost his head over that vixen Lady Ashendon, one couldn't mistake it—but he may come round. Ludovic has got sense too somewhere inside his head. I hope she'll not get engaged to someone else while he does. Ludovic will be back for our wedding, will he not, and Katharine will be your bridesmaid. Well, we shall see."

Katharine had had a sharp tussle with her stepmother on this subject.

One of the most brilliant balls of the season in a large and historic house in London was announced on the day of Lucy's wedding, and Theresa was furious at the idea of Katharine's missing it.

"I work away to get invitations for you," she cried, "and then you do a thing like this."

"Lucy is my greatest friend," said Katharine calmly, "and I want to be her bridesmaid. I hate balls anyhow."

"You are the most ungrateful girl I have ever known, and silly too. All your friends will be there, and James" (James was a very presentable young man who had recently been to stay at Widcote), "and you prefer to be bridesmaid to a little nobody who is marrying an Oxford professor."

"Hullo, what's all this?" said the General, who came into the room closely followed by his spaniel.

"Katharine wants to be bridesmaid to that little Lucy Taynton and if she does that she can't go to the ball at X House. Will you please tell her that this is utter nonsense, she should be seen at this ball."

"Bless my soul," said the General, "Dashbury Park's much more important than any ball in London. I've known Hugh all my life and a Taynton wedding is something I wouldn't miss. Of course Katharine can be bridesmaid and what's more I'll come down to the wedding myself. Lucy's a nice young lady, she likes dogs."

"You can go to the ball by yourself, my dear," he added over his shoulder, "plenty of people to go with. I'd like to see that Taynton girl married to her schoolmaster."

"He's not a schoolmaster, Papa, he's a professor at Oxford," cried Katharine, but the General had left the room.

A few days later Katharine was surprised by her stepmother's interest in her bridesmaid's dress. She was all smiles and graciousness at the thought that Katharine was going to the wedding. Katharine was puzzled by this change of front, until having driven over to see Lucy one afternoon she heard that Ludovic was coming over from Rome to be George Maxwell's best man.

35

Ludovic arrived the day before the wedding. He looked a little older and thinner, and was more silent. But he threw himself into the wedding arrangements and seemed unwilling to discuss his life in Rome or the difficulties of his journey, or his brief sojourn in London. He took charge of the wedding ring, and smiled at Lucy assuring her that all would go well on the following day. He helped Louise, was carefully courteous to Ada and went up and stayed for an hour with his grandmother. A current of sympathy had always flowed between them, but today this was cut off—though neither of them showed it in their manner.

Jane was far too wise ever to force a confidence from anyone. She remarked that Lucy seemed tired.

"Yes," said Ludovic, "and no wonder. You realise, Grandmamma, that she has been sitting up addressing those envelopes of Aunt Ada's till all hours of the night. I shall tell George about it and he will not be pleased."

"No, don't tell him, my dear boy, it will only make him angry with Ada. This work of hers is to her of the first importance and she won't see anything strange in Lucy doing this last bit of work for her. If George speaks coldly to her it will cast a shadow on a day of happiness."

"Well, if you say so, mum's the word, but thank heaven Lucy will be out of all this tomorrow."

"You are quite out of sympathy with Ada," said Jane, her face flushed a faint pink. "Her work for girls and poor women is valuable, more valuable than you know, and she puts it first."

Ludovic's unspoken thought was 'Yes, but Aunt Ada's

up to all sorts of tricks to get her own way, and she tried to prevent Lucy marrying George.'

He glanced at his grandmother. Her face told him nothing, but he received the impression that she knew more about it than he did.

Lucy was sent early to bed. She found Sarah in her room. Sarah was smoothing the sheets on her bed.

"Well, miss," she said, "we shall all miss you—all the others, Bourton and Mrs. Robson say so. You've been a very nice young lady in the house and have made things easy for us. We're glad you are going to marry a good gentleman though he's so quiet."

George and Ludovic sat up talking when Hugh had retired to bed. George noticed some difference in Ludovic. He was quieter for one thing, and laughed less. They sat opposite each other, and the lamps cast a glow on to the tables.

"This is a fine room," said George, breaking the silence.

"Yes," said Ludovic, looking round over his shoulder, "it has good proportions. I like it better than any other room in the house."

George lit his pipe. "Aye," he said deliberately, "you have here a goodly heritage if you choose to take it up."

George had expected an outburst from Ludovic, whose ideas he had constantly heard of and discussed; but Ludovic said nothing for several minutes.

Then, "I wish life wasn't so difficult," he said frowning. "It's such a tangle of loyalties. You're the lucky one, George, your life is straightforward."

"I am indeed lucky," said George gravely. "After to-morrow I shall have a great loyalty and a great responsibility for someone else. In this I rejoice exceedingly. Life without loyalties is a barren, rootless affair, and I can tell you much of my life hitherto has been spent in enduring the sort of quarrels which we breed in colleges for lack of those very things." He smiled briefly, "No, my life in college has not been as peaceful and easy as you imagine."

"No," said Ludovic, staring in front of him, "I don't suppose it has."

The next day was one of sun and shade—a July day with a soft dappled sky. It was warm and colonies of gnats danced in the sunshine and teased the footmen laying tables on the terrace.

The organist in Dashbury played a voluntary and the congregation gazed at the flowers which Mundell had arranged in the church with perhaps more profusion than elegance; they also looked at George's still figure—the nervousness that he felt was masked by his quiet demeanour. Ludovic smiled and the tenantry brought from the Dashbury estates in waggonettes regarded him with even more interest than the bridegroom.

Then framed in a glimpse of the sunshine world outside, Lucy came slowly up the aisle on Hugh's arm, followed equally quietly by Katharine. She did not glance in the direction of Ludovic but received Lucy's bouquet with complete composure, disentangling it from the veil in which it had been momentarily caught. As the service proceeded she kept her eyes on the figures of the bride and bridegroom.

Ludovic stole a glance at Katharine as she stood looking in front of her. Her thoughts were evidently concentrated upon Lucy and on the solemn promises of the Marriage Service as they were pronounced and answered.

Katharine stood for a few moments alone in the aisle when George and Lucy mounted the chancel steps. She looked down at the flowers cradled in her arms, her face remote and quiet and as if shadowed by a secret unhappiness. Ludovic suddenly felt that he would have given much to be able to read her thoughts. She looked up, smiled, and slipped into the pew beside her stepmother and then followed the bridal couple into the vestry.

Later, as Mr. Grainger and his nephew, smartly attired, drove towards Dashbury in a cloud of dust, Mr. Grainger remarked: "You were a fool not to go for that girl, Albert. She looked pretty today, and if you had married her you would have had a better footing at the Park than you'll ever have now. His lordship is settling a little bit of money on her too, and old Ada would have been pleased to have her near to run errands."

His nephew made no reply: he was engaged in brushing his hat, and wondering just how dusty he and his uncle would look when they arrived at the house. He felt and looked cross, for in spite of all his attention and civility he knew that Hugh did not like him, and as for Ludovic, "Conceited puppy," he muttered to himself.

Louise received the guests with grace and a welcoming smile. Earlier in the day she had been stung by a gnat and the bite had swollen half-way through the afternoon. It felt hot and irritating and made the bracelet on her arm tight and uncomfortable. Louise always wore a heavy gold bracelet with links which joined in a centre shaped like a locket in which was embedded a diamond spray of flowers. She was never parted from it—Hugh had given it to her on their marriage and it had belonged to his grandmother.

She had been stung on the left arm just where the bracelet fitted above her wrist. Her other wrist had already an imposing pair of bracelets, but she unclasped it and slipped it on below the two others. One of the guests called her attention away as she was standing in the hall, so that she did not notice she had not fastened it securely. It slid down her skirt and was swept under a red leather chair by the voluminous skirt of a lady who was passing.

Attended by Katharine, Lucy came downstairs in her going-away dress at that moment and all attention was focused on her and George, who awaited her. Lucy said her farewells and they walked together into the porch. She was embraced by Louise and grasped in a strong handshake by Hugh; while even Ada went so far as to give her an embarrassed hug.

The two mounted into the carriage, en route for the station, to journey to London, where the kind McAndrews had put their house at their disposal for a few days.

Katharine standing on the steps of the pillared porch looked at Lucy's shyly radiant face and George's graver countenance, which indicated relief at being free of the wedding festivities. She turned with a little sigh to find Ludovic beside her.

"Would you care for a walk?" he asked.

Katharine, startled, said, "Yes, but I must change first."

"I will wait by the fountain," he replied.

<hr>

36

HUGH had departed to his room. He announced that he would shortly go up to the kitchen garden to see about something there.

Presently Katharine appeared and slowly descended the steps of the terrace. Ludovic had been looking down into the waters of the fountain. He raised his head and asked, "Where is the General?"

"He is talking to Lady Dashbury before going back to

Widcote. It's nearly all shut up, but there's someone there to look after him. He says he would rather be there than in London going to a ball."

"I don't blame him," said Ludovic. "I've had enough of balls myself."

Katharine looked at him with a smile. "Aren't you rather young to say that?"

"I don't feel at all young," said Ludovic sombrely.

"I wish I didn't," said Katharine. "I should like to know a lot more than I do. I don't like London, I love the country, but I've learnt a lot of things in London. I've seen pictures and plays, and," she added in a lower voice, "I've learnt just how nasty and sometimes how nice people can be."

"Do you have to go there?"

"Yes, my stepmother loves it. She likes crowds and fashionable people."

They walked under the tunnel overhung by bushes.

"Let's sit down," said Ludovic, "you must be tired."

"I am a little, but I am so glad about Lucy that I don't feel it. She is the best person I know and she is so happy."

"Yes, they should be very well suited to each other." He stopped and Katharine said to break the silence: "Lucy says that George has his eye on a little house. It's got pointed windows and balconies, and she laughed and said that she believed the basement was full of black beetles, but even so she thought it perfect."

Katharine remained very still remembering the sharp unhappiness of the last time she had sat on that seat, while Violet had talked to Ludovic by the fountain.

She glanced at Ludovic. He was making patterns in the dust with a stick, frowning down at the ground. He was about to speak, but remained silent and leaned back against the seat. She closed her eyes for a moment. After the mixed emotions of the day of pleasure and discomfort,

Katharine felt her own private unhappiness mounting, but she showed no outward disturbance. Ludovic said, his voice a little rough and uneven:

"All that happened here in the spring is over and done with. I want to assure you of that. I feel I must say this as you were here and saw me being made a fool of, and behaving like a fool. I want to tell you, too, that it's all over now on my side. There was never anything on hers. I didn't see that she was only amusing herself." He took up the stick again and added to the pattern he had made in the dust. "I went back to Rome unhappy, furiously angry with her. Everything seemed like this dust." He obliterated the pattern, sending a fine powdery whirl up into the air. "I must have been intolerable in Rome. I disliked everything and everybody there. Then I grew more and more ashamed of myself. I had been so foolish and so unkind."

"Unkind?"

"Yes, unkind to everyone. I had hurt my grandmother who is a saint, and, above all, I had hurt Uncle Hugh. He found Violet with me at night in the drawing-room, I was begging her to go away with me and she was refusing. There was nothing else. He behaved with great restraint the next morning, but I burst out and said I didn't want this place or any responsibility or money or anything. He was deeply hurt, I could see. But wrapped up in my own furious anger and humiliation, I did not know what I had done to him. But then I thought it over and indeed I have thought of nothing else since then, and now . . ." he paused. Katharine turned to him; there were tears in her eyes.

"Poor Ludovic, poor Lord Dashbury."

Ludovic looked at her, then resumed his pattern, the stick shaking slightly in his hand.

"I am determined to make amends. I shall ask him to see me tomorrow morning and . . . and tell him that in future I shall come here as much as I can to learn about this place and some day take it over from him, and that all his hard work won't have been in vain."

Katharine's face lit up. "That is wonderful," she said. "I know you are making a great sacrifice: you wanted to be free."

Ludovic shook his head. "Nobody's free," he said. "I saw that when I began to think things over clearly. You can't be in this world. It's better to have work to do and to try to carry on what your ancestors have worked for. I sound a bit of a prig but perhaps one has got to be a bit priggish at times."

"I don't think you sound priggish," said Katharine. "I think you are absolutely right." She turned to him: "And you will have happy times here in this place."

He looked at her and said,

"Katharine, would you help me? Would you consider marrying me?"

Katharine flushed deeply. "But," she stammered, "you don't love me."

"Yes, I do. I realised it when I was in Rome. My thoughts always came back to you, when I was at my sorest and angriest, and it gave me a feeling of peace. I felt that if you ever could care for me, we could be happy. I would give you all I've got to give if you will say yes. But I don't suppose you can after all that's happened."

"Yes," said Katharine, "I've always cared for you since I first saw you."

It was some time before they left the shrubbery. There was so much to recount, so many things to be said, so many doubts to be vanquished. They finally emerged and paced towards the fountain, into the soft and radiant evening. Ludovic lifted up his face to the house and turned his head towards the landscape, and then looked at Katharine and smiled. They paused by the fountain and were mounting the terrace when Hugh's dog Jester bolted out through the french window and ran quickly round the house in the direction of the stables. There was something hurried and furtive in his gait.

Soey had taken a look out of the window.

"Mr. Ludovic and Miss Katharine are out there, m'lady," she announced.

"Are they really?" said Jane faintly. The excitements of the day had tired her, but she put up a silent prayer to heaven for Ludovic's happiness.

≈≈≈≈≈ 37 ≈≈≈≈≈

JESTER had had a very dull day. He had been immured in the gun room while the wedding was going on and had been forgotten until Bourton released him in the late afternoon. His canine mind was full of a sense of grievance. He found his way into the hall. It was empty now of people. He heard distant voices and made his way towards them, wagging his tail. He was extremely hungry and as he neared the drawing-room door he saw a plateful of small and succulent-looking cakes on a stool near the pagodas. The footmen had been clearing away the food on the tables on the terrace, and the second footman in a moment of flurry had put down the cakes meaning to return and take them back to the still-room. But something distracted his attention and he had forgotten to come back.

Jester loved cakes as much as he loved anything in the

204

world and was seldom allowed them, as his girth was increasing. He put his paws up on the stool and seized one and then another. As he nosed about for one last cake the plate tipped, slid under the arm of the chair, and crashed on to the floor. It shivered into pieces and Jester, knowing that retribution would certainly overtake him if he were found by the scene of his crime, ran quickly through the drawing-room and, seeing the advancing figures of Ludovic and Katharine, dodged and ran round the house as fast as he could. Several crumbs clung to his muzzle but the cakes had been delicious and he had no regrets.

Hugh had been for a walk and come back feeling satisfied with the day's work. He sincerely rejoiced in Lucy and George's marriage. He had given her as good a send-off as a member of the Taynton family could have, and he reminded himself that he must congratulate Mrs. Robson on the excellence of the food, and Bourton for all the extra work he had put in. He had hardly spoken to Ludovic but had been conscious that his nephew had been helping by talking to dull neighbours and seeing to the wants of everyone, and that in the brief moments they had been together there had been a sort of eagerness to please in Ludovic's manner towards him. Ludovic seemed different somehow.

Hugh put down his hat and prepared to make his way to see if Louise, Katharine and Ludovic were in the drawing-room or outside. He suddenly caught sight of the broken plate and the scattered cakes which Jester had not eaten. With an exclamation of annoyance he stooped down to look more closely and his eyes caught the glitter of gold. He drew Louise's bracelet out from underneath the chair.

Contact with the marble floor had broken several of the gold links but the diamond device on the locket had remained uninjured. He turned it over. The thin gold sheath at the back was also intact, but its hinges were broken and it fell apart in his hand. He took it into his room and put it carefully on the writing table. As he took it up the back fell out. Inside was another sheet of gold. He remembered that years ago there was a little sliding catch almost invisible, a sort of trick to open it. It was whispered, he remembered, that his grandmother, a gay lady, was said to have kept the portrait or a lock of the hair of her current lover in there. When he had given it to Louise he recalled showing her this tiny catch and they had laughed about it together. His fingers found it and he pressed it. The thin gold plate opened widely and he saw a small miniature of a man whose face he had known since boyhood. The miniature, loosened by the shock of the fall on to the marble floor, fell a little forward. He carefully prised it out. On the back of the locket was written 'Roddy to Louise' and a date. He sat down heavily and laid the bracelet back on the writing table in front of him.

Roddy to Louise. The date was two years before. Hugh got up heavily and walked into the hall. The visitors' book stood on the table. He took it back into his room and turned back the pages. He found an entry and compared the date with that on the miniature. They matched exactly. He shut the book, went out, replaced it on the hall table, and came back and sat down again at his desk.

His first feeling was of furious anger, hurt and disgust, succeeded by a deadly depression. The day had been a happy but fatiguing one. He had been really anxious for Lucy's sake that all should go well. He knew that his temper had been irritable in the morning. He had snapped at Ada when she wanted to alter the time of the carriages to come round. But he had shown a smiling face to his guests, and the memory of George's deserved happiness and Lucy's smile came back to him. "Let's hope," he said half-aloud, "there will be no ugly surprises in their married life." He put his head in his hands. What was there to do? Roddy had been drowned in a sailing accident on the Riviera. He had grieved for his old schoolfellow and had sorely missed his visits to Dashbury and their meetings in London.

Roddy and Louise: it was inconceivable. He said the two names aloud. Louise had always behaved with so much dignity; she had never indulged in the easy flirtations or romantic friendships so dear to her women friends. In spite of her undoubted good looks she had never attracted attention to herself or given cause for a breath of scandal to touch her name. Roddy had lived a life of racing, sailing and hunting. He was the owner of large property and of sufficient money for all the good things of the world. He had a name for being pursued by many women, but if he pursued in return he kept the matter very quiet, and was evasive in a debonair sort of way, brushing aside with a joke enquiries as to the state of his heart or the depth of his feelings. Hugh was accustomed to keeping his own emotions under the strictest control. In his heart of hearts he despised people who showed any kind of strong feeling, and now he was consumed by anger that his greatest friend and his wife should have carried on an intrigue under his own roof, behind his back. He walked about the room into which the July evening was showing a little hint of the decline from high summer. In spite of the calm blueness of the sky, in which floated long placid narrow white clouds, there was a hint that autumn was not many months away. The thoughts followed each other in a remorseless sequence through Hugh's head. When and where had they met? Roddy had a small and well-appointed house in London. Had Louise gone there to see him? Surely someone, the servants, anyhow, would have noticed and talked. Had they in fact done so and were all his friends laughing to themselves at him? Hugh, the successful man who understood banking and yet was a country gentleman and a fine sportsman. He knew that his sarcastic tongue had not endeared him to many people, and that not suffering fools with any show of gladness or even tolerance he had made enemies—enemies who would be only too delighted to hear that he had been deceived by his wife and his friend. He would never be able to walk into his club without wondering whether the talk which stopped abruptly when he entered had been gossip about his private affairs.

He tried to remember how Louise had taken the news of Roddy's death. Away at the time, he had returned to find a house party at Dashbury. Louise had listened in silence while people talked about Roddy. She had been as usual punctilious in her duties as hostess. He recalled that when the guests had departed she had pleaded the excuse that she had a bad headache and had remained in her darkened bedroom with a handkerchief steeped in eau-de-Cologne over her forehead. Her headaches seemed to have got worse in recent years, he remembered; and her visits to church more frequent. He had never interfered with her churchgoing, and had spoken sharply to Ada who said that the church Louise attended in London had Popish practices.

His thoughts were becoming well-nigh intolerable. He took a large envelope out of his writing-table drawer and put the bracelet into it, and the little miniature into a smaller envelope, then put them both in his pocket.

As he was crossing the hall he noticed the retreating figure of Louise's maid slipping through a doorway on the left, while to the right beyond the pagodas Soey emerged. She advanced towards him. "Her ladyship would like to see you, m'lord, she says, if you could spare the time."

Hugh started. His thoughts were so pressing that he'd almost become unconscious of his surroundings and his feet trod the marble floor with no feeling of its hardness. Soey turned and he followed her.

When he reached his mother's room he found her propped up with pillows, a flush upon her cheeks.

"My dear Hugh," she said, "this is selfish of me. I know it's been a long day for you, but Louise has gone to her room and Ada is completely uncommunicative. I don't know where Ludovic is. I wanted just to hear from you how everything went."

Hugh sat down heavily. The wedding seemed very far away. He frowned and tried to bring his mind back to it.

"It went off very satisfactorily, I think," he said. "No, there wasn't a hitch. Everything was punctual, the church was full, the tea was good, we had it on the terrace." Then he stopped (the smashed plateful of cakes, the links of the bracelet). He leaned back in the chair unable to say anything more. He took out his handkerchief and wiped his forehead.

"Hugh," said his mother, "forgive my bothering you. You look so tired. Do you feel ill?"

"It's been rather a heavy day," he said. He spoke slowly and with difficulty. "But I'm always glad to come and see you."

"I think you do feel unwell or," said his mother anxiously, "you haven't had bad news, have you? Lucy and George didn't have a carriage accident on the way to the station?"

"No, no, Marston came back some time ago from the station."

A sudden wave of unhappiness and loneliness overcame him as he stared at his mother's anxious face. "I found this," he said, and he took the two envelopes out of his pocket. He laid them on the shawl which covered Jane Dashbury.

"Louise's bracelet," she said.

o   209

He nodded briefly.

Jane carefully slid the bracelet out of the envelope. "Oh dear, it's broken, but it can be mended." There was a note of anxiety in her voice, of fear, more than concern about a broken bracelet would warrant. She slid the miniature out of the other envelope and turned it over.

"You found this?"

He told her what had happened and she listened, holding the miniature in her hand. Something in her look and silence stung Hugh into speech. "Did you know of this, Mother?"

There was a silence in the room. Jane looked down at the bracelet and the miniature.

"I knew nothing for certain," Jane said slowly. "I just ... Yes, I suppose I did know, though no one ever told me anything, but I noticed little things, Louise looking happy at times, cast down at others, and then Soey had to come and tell me that she had seen them go to the Temple and stay there for a long time. I have tried to check Soey's habit of looking out of the window and repeating what she sees to me, but she comes and says it before I have time to stop her, and then she says she's sorry and does it again next time."

"It wasn't only Soey," she added. "Mary Parker told me that she had seen them together talking earnestly in a remote part of Hyde Park when she happened by chance to be walking there, and other little things like straws in the wind."

"Do you think many people know?"

"No," said his mother, "I don't, and as Roddy is dead any gossip will be soon forgotten in some new talk about somebody else. Forget about that side of it and think now what you must do."

"You mean I must go to Louise and tax her with this?"

210

"I don't mean that at all. Just give me a minute or two to think."

She laid the bracelet and the miniature on the table beside her, and put her head back on the pillow and closed her eyes. Her lips moved a little.

"Hugh," she said, "you must do this. You must go to Louise and tell her what you have found. She is probably in an agony of mind at this moment. Her maid is probably searching everywhere for the bracelet."

"Oh, yes, I saw her in the hall."

"No doubt of it. You must tell Louise about it, however painful it is to you both."

"It is extremely painful to me. I never thought, I never guessed. I wondered in passing once or twice why she always wore this bracelet when she had so many others, but I never thought it was a hiding place for her lover's picture. No one, of course, knew of the secret catch except yourself and me, and I had forgotten about it till now. . . ."

Jane Dashbury raised herself on her pillow and said softly: "Hugh, I am going to say something which gives me pain and will give you pain too. You have no right to be harsh with your wife."

"Please, Mother, leave what I once did out of this."

"I cannot do so, you broke your marriage vow with someone who was all charm and beauty, and whom in spite of everything I loved. Louise heard about it and never said a word to anyone but the hurt went very deep with her. And then you became, not more kindly and understanding, but harsh and cold and more aloof as the years went on. Your marriage was a sham, a façade, there was no warmth or feeling in it. You both retreated behind good manners and decorum and Louise felt it deeply. Then Roddy came along, all gallantry and sympathetic charm, and he gave her that flattering interest in all she did and the affection that she did not get from you. Look into your heart and see where the blame lies. You can share it between you; you have both much to forgive each other."

Hugh sat frowning at her, his mouth drawn in a tight line.

"It grieves me to speak like this. I should have spoken earlier. I tried to help Louise but she erected so high a barrier between herself and me that I could never break it down. Hugh," she said urgently, "you and Louise have a chance now of being happier than you have been for years. If you can have truth between you, you can build on that. I beg of you, don't lose this chance, it will never come again. You are my only son and I would give all I possess and much more to see you and Louise in a fair way to be happier before I die. Hugh, you have always been upright. I know that you have been kind and generous to people poorer than yourself. Summon up all your generosity, forgive Louise, be sorry for what you once did to her. Make your respect for her grow into affection and trust. After all, she has been a very good wife to you. She has managed this house in such a way that an invitation to stay here is valued as a compliment. She has been respected in London society for her good breeding and good manners. Remember all this."

Hugh rose heavily to his feet.

"Go now, Hugh, this minute," said his mother. She held the bracelet and miniature in her hands and he took them from her.

"Very well," he said.

When he had closed the door Jane Dashbury's head fell back on to the pillow. The strain had told on her heart and she rang her bell for Soey, who, clucking and grumbling, gave her restoratives.

Hugh walked slowly along the passage until he reached the gallery round the top of the hall. He passed slowly along it, looking down for a moment into its depths. Then he walked on resolutely and knocked at the door of his wife's room.

She called out, "Come in," and he entered and shut the door behind him.

Louise was standing in the middle of the room. She was still wearing her smart wedding dress. Her hair was disordered and she had been crying.

She stared at Hugh. "Has anything gone wrong?" she said. "Did you want me?" Her voice was rough and uneven.

"A lot has gone wrong," said Hugh, "but perhaps it can be put right."

He took the two envelopes out of his pocket and handed her the contents.

She took them and her face whitened. "What are you going to do?" she said.

"Nothing," said Hugh, "except to say that I am sorry."

Louise fumbled her way to an armchair and sat down. She was shaking all over.

"We have both got a great deal to reproach ourselves with," said Hugh, "but don't let's reproach each other. If you are willing to forget my past, I will forget yours."

Louise frowned, not in anger but in bewilderment.

"You're very generous and you're kind," she said in a strangled voice. "I don't understand . . ."

Hugh sat down in the nearest chair.

"Try and understand, and I will try and explain. I have been talking to my mother . . ."

"Your mother?"

"Yes, she never tells what she hears." He leant forward. "She has talked to me very sternly about myself and has shown me in a not at all pleasant light. It's not very agreeable to be told of one's omissions and faults, but what she

213

said was not undeserved. I have failed to give you the affection which was your due as my wife. I loved someone else and when she died the remembrance of her didn't help me to be better and kinder. I just hardened my heart against everyone and everything." He paused. "It wasn't perhaps surprising that you sought what I didn't give you elsewhere."

Louise sat with her hands tightly pressed together.

Hugh continued: "The two people we loved are dead and I at least am anxious to make amends and to try and make our marriage a happier one. Will you try too?"

"I will," said Louise. "I will try: it's a lot of it my fault. But when I realised about Dorothy I was so hurt and miserable. I longed to tell you that I would forgive you if you would turn to me, but you were so frozen and I became frozen too, and Roddy brought something into my life. He made me enjoy everything and I hadn't enjoyed anything for a long time, Hugh." Tears were pouring down her face faster than she could dry them. "I've wanted to tell you. I went to confession in London. Ada doesn't know, but I did and I confessed everything, and Father Francis told me that I must tell you the truth, he said that otherwise I should be living a lie. I meant to tell you that day when I said to you that there wasn't much happiness about. I really did mean to, though I was terrified when I said it, and then you went away and shut the door. And then there never seemed to be a right moment to speak. I promised the Father I would tell you and I meant it, I really did mean to keep my promise."

"Don't cry," said Hugh.

"I'll try not to, I know you hate tears. I will try and do better in future."

Hugh looked intently at her. Her tears had fallen on to her light-coloured taffeta dress where they made dark stains. Her handkerchief was a crumpled wisp, her eyes were puffy with crying, and a lock of hair had fallen loosely on to her shoulder. Hugh felt more moved by her piteous defeated look than he had for years by the elegant finish of her appearance.

"Try and rest," he said. "It's been a long, hard day."

"No," she said. "I shall come down to dinner. It's just as hard for you."

"We will talk again tomorrow, my dear."

38

DINNER that evening was a strange meal. Ludovic and Katharine hardly heard what was said to them and answered at random. And to any two people less preoccupied with their own thoughts than Hugh and Louise it would have been obvious that they had reached some kind of understanding. Ludovic pulled himself together and tried to talk and Katharine came out of a happy dream to make some shy observations, but all conversation seemed to end abruptly in a silence which pervaded the long, ornate room. A moth fluttered in from the garden on to one of the candle shades on the table, and Ludovic, moving quickly to save it, and to take it and throw it outside, upset the candlestick and the shade went on fire. It was promptly quenched and removed by Bourton but even this diversion did not lighten the atmosphere.

Hugh did not linger over the port wine. He rose, and said to Louise: "I must go and see my mother. Will you come?" And they left the dining-room together.

"What on earth is up?" said Ludovic. "Anyway, it needn't bother us. Let's go outside for a moment."

When Hugh and Louise reached Jane's bedroom, Soey opened the door with a look of doom on her face.

"Her ladyship had one of her queer turns after you left her, m'lord."

Hugh walked into the room. Jane, frail and exhausted, looked at him. When Soey left the room he said: "I've done what you asked me, Mother."

Louise came up to the side of the bed and said in a steady voice: "Hugh has been very good to me."

"I am so thankful," said Jane, "and now, my dears, try and go on being good."

"I'm going to try," said Louise, "and try hard. I'm so grateful, Mamma, you've always been . . ." Her voice choked.

"We had better go," said Hugh, "she can't stand any more."

He went into the next room. Soey gave him an angry glance.

"I think we should send for the doctor," he said.

"Her ladyship won't hear of it," said Soey tartly. "I've wanted to do it these two hours past but she's taken the drops he gave her and she says all she wants is rest."

Hugh went back into his mother's room. "I hear you won't have the doctor."

Jane smiled. "I don't want to see him," she said. "My mind is easier than it has been for years."

Hugh stooped and kissed her thin cheek.

39

THE doctor came early the next morning and pronounced Jane Dashbury's condition quite satisfactory; in fact she was better, he thought, than when he had last seen her. Soey heard his opinion with mixed feelings. She had wanted Hugh to feel conscience-stricken that he had upset her mistress, and on the other hand she was glad that she was better. The gloom of her face didn't noticeably relax. She merely remarked to Jane that she hoped that she wouldn't allow his lordship to worry her again, to which Jane replied, "That will do, Soey, please give me my book."

Ludovic waited in the drawing-room watching for the doctor's departure through the open door. When Hugh turned back to walk to his room Ludovic emerged and followed him to his study.

The events of the day before had taken their toll of Hugh. His shoulders looked a little bowed. He sat in his chair more loosely than usual and looked up at his nephew.

"If you have anything to say will you say it quickly, please, as I have a lot to do and think about this morning."

Hugh braced himself to stare at Ludovic, who bore an aspect at once serious and eager as he hesitated as to how to begin what he had got to say.

Hugh had been pleased the day before by Ludovic's behaviour. He had talked to dull neighbours and had seen that they were well supplied with refreshment, and he had also talked to each of the people from the estate, who were being regaled with more solid fare upon tables spread in front of the house. More than that, he had looked as if he had liked doing it.

"I'm afraid that what I've got to say is all rather long and complicated, Uncle Hugh. I want first of all to tell you that I have changed my mind, and that, if you still wish it, I would like to be your heir not only in name but in fact. I've come to see things differently and in a clearer light," and he went on more rapidly, "If you will put me in the way of learning things here I will give my mind and shoulder my responsibilities as you wanted me to do."

Hugh looked at him but did not speak.

"I know," continued Ludovic, "that you must find this change very astonishing, but perhaps you could forget our last talk on the subject, and let me try and make a fresh start?"

"I am very glad to hear all this," said Hugh, "but it seems rather sudden. Are you sure that you mean all you say?"

"Yes, I paced up and down in my room in Rome night after night and gradually I saw things clearer," and he added, "George Maxwell thinks that rootless people aren't much good."

"Sensible man."

"Will you give me a try?"

"Of course I will," said Hugh. "I haven't had time to think about it, but I am very glad about this."

"And then," said Ludovic with some embarrassment, "something else very important has happened. I have asked Katharine to marry me and she has consented. With her I can face anything in the future."

"You really want to marry her?"

"Yes, indeed I do," and there was a ring in Ludovic's voice which convinced his hearer.

"May I go and fetch her?"

Hugh nodded. When Ludovic left the room Hugh put his head in his hands. So much had happened in the last twenty-four hours that his mind refused to grasp it all. Was there just a hope that the road ahead, although not smooth, and often uphill, would lead to some measure of happiness?

At that moment he heard footsteps outside and Ludovic and Katharine came in hand-in-hand.

Epilogue

THE Dashbury family were altered by the events related in the preceding chapter; outward and inward pressures had changed them.

Lucy soon settled down to her life in Oxford, and Ludovic and Katharine were married in the early autumn. Theresa Wilson Fyfield insisted on a London wedding. Her jubilations over Katharine's marriage strained the patience of all those to whom she talked.

Katharine from never being right could now do no wrong, for was she not marrying a man who would succeed to title, money and a large estate? Katharine at first tried to keep Ludovic and her stepmother as much apart as possible, but she discovered that Ludovic took her snobberies with good-humoured amusement.

The General was in his remote and abrupt way delighted with his daughter's marriage. He hoped to see more dogs in Dashbury. He wished to present Katharine with a finely bred spaniel puppy, but she reminded him that she and Ludovic would not be at Dashbury all the time and also that Jester would not welcome a newcomer.

Albert Grainger threw up his job at Dashbury. He did not get on with Hugh, and saw that he would never be tolerated by Ludovic. Old Mr. Grainger was disappointed, but no one else minded his leaving; he had been written down as an impertinent upstart by all the Dashbury neighbourhood.

Jane went back to the Dower House, where she grew a little stronger and enjoyed her garden, and Lucy and George's visits.

Ada announced that she had settled to live in London. She had realised that when Lucy left she would get no more help with her voluminous correspondence. She was arranging to share a small house in Chelsea with a friend equally devoted to good works, and who knew of a young lady who would help with secretarial work. She would of course often visit Dashbury Park and the Dower House. Jane drew a breath of relief when this was settled. She felt that Ada would live in a circle of people who would appreciate her organising ability and her desire to help her fellow men and women. Moreover she would sometimes have to yield her opinions to those of other people, and in the larger world of London she would not command the prestige of Miss Taynton of Dashbury.

Ludovic and Katharine were well suited to each other and her steadiness of character enabled Ludovic to pursue the various avocations to which he addressed himself, while she taught him gently to laugh at himself and not to treat the difficulties of life and the boredom of routine with undue seriousness.

Perhaps a hint might be given that George Maxwell became eventually head of his college in Oxford and that Alastair McAndrew received high legal office.

Lucy and George's happiness deepened and increased through the years, and Hugh and Louise drew nearer together. They were wise enough to see that they had come to a turning point in their lives, and that their life together now could come to have a deeper meaning. Hugh found that Louise gave him an unexpected sympathy in his work, and he showed her a kindness and a lack of brusqueness when he talked matters over with her. Each had much to forget about the other, but they wisely put thoughts of the past behind them, and Dashbury Park had a mellower atmosphere.

The day of Ludovic and Katharine's wedding the house was emptier than it had been for years. Jane had gone to the Dower House and Bourton, Sarah and Mrs. Robson had all been transported to London for the ceremony. The under-servants were in charge.

The house stood quietly waiting for more dramas to be enacted, for the cries of joy and anger of children, for guests driving up to the pillared porch and after a while driving away again, for all the rubs and harshnesses of daily life and its moments of sweetness and understanding, its false starts and recoveries.

The motes of dust danced in the slanting sunlight of the hall and Jester ran across it on some errand of his own.